Romeo

Single Dad Society

Delaney Diamond

Garden Avenue Press

Romeo by Delaney Diamond

Garden Avenue Press

Atlanta, Georgia

978-1-946302-34-2 (Ebook edition)

978-1-946302-35-9 (Paperback edition)

www.delaneydiamond.com

Chapter 1

Marcus

I looked at the woman sleeping peacefully beside me.

Jackie.

My arm was numb, and I had to figure out how to get out of her bed without waking her up.

Slowly, carefully, I eased my arm from under her back. She moaned in her sleep and shifted position. I froze and waited. As I held my breath, she rolled onto her side, away from me.

Hallelujah.

My arm was free but tingling. I flexed my fingers and then slowly sat up, keeping an eye on her to make sure I didn't wake her from her sleep.

I moved quietly through the bedroom, gathering my clothes from the trail we had left between the closed door and the bed. My jeans were on the chair in the corner, and my shirt crumpled in a pile on top of my shoes at the foot of the bed. Somehow, one of my socks ended up next to the nightstand. I almost didn't see it because it was black.

I dressed quietly, glancing at her sleeping form every now and then. She had auburn hair and light brown skin. We had a great night after meeting at The Flight Club, where my Alpha Phi Alpha brothers and I hung out every month. She was beautiful and funny, but I had to get out of there because I knew what would happen.

She'd invite me to stay for breakfast, and over breakfast she'd ask a bunch of questions. Nothing out of the ordinary—just the type of questions you would ask someone you had recently slept with. But I wouldn't have the answers she wanted. I wasn't looking for anything serious, and most of the time, that's what women expected when they let you inside their bodies.

So it was better for me to go, slipping away in the early morning before she woke up.

I found a napkin inside my jacket pocket and scribbled a note: *Thanks for a great time. Take care. —Romeo*

I cringed. I never knew what message to leave but hated ducking out without a word and used my line name as a cover.

I slipped out of the room and eased the door shut. My shoes barely made a sound as I walked across her hardwood floors to the front door. I let myself out, making sure to turn the lock on the inside before shutting the door.

Once outside, I breathed easier and relaxed. In the crisp, early morning spring air, I checked my phone on the way to my blue Toyota Rav4. Last night, my frat brother Jashaun had texted me a link about upcoming zoning changes and followed up this morning with additional information. Since he worked for the city, he was always giving me the heads up about what was coming down the pike in local real estate, which was very helpful in my work as an agent.

I hit him back real quick and then climbed behind the wheel. I drove through the city that I'd been living in since I graduated from Prairieview University eleven years ago. My plan had been to find an entry-level corporate job and work my way up to executive one day. After only a few months, I realized that wasn't the path for me.

A couple of years later, I earned my real estate license, and for the past five years, I had been in the top one percent of real estate agents in the state, closing millions of dollars' worth of deals every month.

As I neared my condo, my phone rang. I didn't recognize the number on the screen, but it could've been an old client calling with a referral or some other type of business, so I answered.

"Marcus Hayes," I said.

"Hello, Mr. Hayes. My name is Julia Richmond," a pleasant-sounding female voice said.

"Hello, Ms. Richmond. How can I help you?" My mind was already on breakfast. After I went home, I planned to walk to the café near my place and have coffee and a sausage, egg, and cheese bagel—my weekend ritual—before heading into the real estate office.

"I work for Safe Harbor Child Advocacy, a non-profit organization that partners with CPS. I'm calling about Brandon and Stacey Mitchell."

My stomach tightened as I slowed to a stop at a red light. Brandon Mitchell was my best friend. Stacey was his wife.

"Did something happen?" The question came out steady, but I gripped the steering wheel as fear enveloped me.

"I'm very sorry to inform you, Mr. Hayes, that Brandon and Stacey were involved in an accident three nights ago. A drunk driver hit them head-on, and they were both pronounced dead at the scene."

What?

My heart stopped. Brandon and Stacey were dead? I must not have heard her correctly. I talked to Brandon on Monday, and last week I was at his house helping him put up curtain rods because Stacey threatened to divorce him if he didn't get it done.

My lungs stopped working.

The woman with the pleasant voice continued speaking, explaining something about not suffering, but I heard her words in a haze. My brain hadn't moved on from the devastating information that my friends were dead.

Dead.

"Mr. Hayes? Are you there?"

I snapped out of my temporary coma. At the same time, the driver behind me honked his horn irritably.

I swallowed and pressed the accelerator. "Yeah. I'm here."

"The reason I'm calling is because of my role as a child advocate. The Mitchells have a son, Noah, and he's been with the babysitter this entire time. Because he was left without a legal guardian unexpectedly, CPS was notified," she explained gently. "I was assigned to Noah's case. My job is to monitor his transition into your care and make sure he has access to grief and trauma services while we sort out his family situation."

"Brandon and Stacey don't have family here," I said in a robotic voice.

"So we've come to learn. Brandon does have a sister who is willing to take the boy. She lives in Tennessee. The babysitter is unable to keep him long-term, so until his aunt can get here—"

"Where is he?" I pulled over, parking in an empty slot at the front of my building. Poor Noah. I can't imagine what he must be feeling.

"As I said, he's with the babysitter. Would you like the address?"

"Yes."

He was probably with Mrs. Patterson. I knew her name but not where she lived. I pulled out the same pen I had used earlier to write the note to Jackie.

She gave me the address, and my hand shook the entire time I wrote down the information.

"Are you able to pick him up today?"

"Yeah, I can get him. I'll leave right now."

"That's good. Mr. Hayes—"

"Call me Marcus," I said automatically—something I did often in my line of work to put clients at ease. Being formal implied distance between us. Using first names created the sense that we were working on the house sale or purchase together as a team.

"Marcus," the pleasant voice said. "I want you to know that I'm here if you need assistance navigating the resources available for you and Noah. My role as an advocate means I'll be checking in periodically to see how you're managing and make sure Noah is doing well too. Once you're settled, please give me a call in the next day or two so we can meet. I'd like to do an evaluation and discuss next steps."

We talked for a few more minutes, and then I ended the call. Though I told her I would leave right away, I didn't. I sat there, letting the tragedy sink in. My best friend and his wife were gone, and now I was responsible for a seven-year-old kid who was waiting for someone to come get him.

I was Noah's godfather and had said yes when Brandon asked me to be his guardian should anything happen to him and Stacey. But deep down, I never thought anything would actually happen to them. Now, sitting in the car with the engine off and the morning sun climbing higher in the sky, the reality of the situation was setting in.

I had agreed to be responsible for a child. A grieving, traumatized human being who had lost both of his parents.

I had a two-bedroom condo and a job that sometimes required me to work nights and weekends, but I didn't have to worry about anyone but myself. I couldn't cook, and most of the time, I ate out. Anyone checking my cabinets would be appalled at the amount of unhealthy food on the shelves.

All of that would have to change, at least temporarily. I didn't know what seven-year-olds ate, what time they were supposed to go to bed, and how the hell to talk to someone who had lost both their parents at such a young age.

I should probably get the contact information for Noah's aunt in Tennessee. But that's not what I did. I agreed to pick him up, and I could at least do that while I figured out what the next steps would be.

Starting the car again, I pulled into traffic, heading down the highway on my way to pick up Noah.

Chapter 2

Marcus

As I drove home, I checked the rearview mirror, my gaze landing on Noah in the booster seat behind me. He wore a Robin costume, complete with the mask, which he refused to take off. I had tried to get him to wear regular clothes once, but he looked at me with the biggest, saddest eyes and simply said, "I don't want to."

I immediately gave up.

Right now, his eyes were downcast, and he clutched an action figure in his left hand.

We had just left my real estate office. I was taking him everywhere with me because I didn't want to leave him alone with anyone else since I was worried about him feeling abandoned.

I knew taking care of him would be a challenge, but I had no idea how much. I already felt as if I was failing. Miserably.

Four days ago, I received a phone call from Julia Richmond, and my life changed. While processing the fact that my best friend was gone, I was stumbling through this guardian role.

When I picked up Noah, the babysitter—Mrs. Patterson—had warned me that he wasn't talking much or eating either. Since then, I had tried everything I could think of.

I gave him cereal, Pop Tarts, chicken nuggets, mini pizzas, and other food I believed kids enjoyed—some I remembered him eating whenever I spent time with him and his dad, Brandon. But all he did was take a bite or two and then push the plate away. If I didn't figure out something soon, the kid might die of malnutrition.

"Do you want to get something to eat? We can get hotdogs." Personally, I wasn't hungry, but I figured he might be. He hadn't eaten much of the cereal I gave him this morning and had only eaten a couple of chips for lunch.

"Okay." He answered in a dull, lifeless voice.

He might take two bites and then be done, but I was hoping he would eat more than that. All kids liked hotdogs, didn't they?

My phone rang, and this time I recognized the number, though I hadn't saved her name. It was Julia, the child advocate. *Crap*. I had forgotten to call her.

Instead of putting her on speaker as I normally would when I was alone in the car, I stuck my Bluetooth in my ear and answered. "Marcus Hayes." I sounded as lifeless and dull as Noah did.

"Hello, Marcus. It's Julia Richmond, the child advocate. We spoke a few days ago, and I'm checking to see how you and Noah are doing." Thankfully, her voice wasn't accusatory.

I glanced at the rearview mirror. Noah sat with slumped shoulders, head bent, a slight furrow on his brow. What was he thinking about?

"We're... managing," I answered, hoping she could read between the lines.

"Managing. Okay," she said, in a way that made me suspect

she fully understood that I was struggling. "As I explained during our first conversation, I'd like to assess how Noah is adjusting to his new environment. Are you at home right now?"

"Actually, I'm on the road. I just left my office, and he's with me."

"In that case, would it be too much trouble for you to stop by my office? There's a park across the street, and we can go there to be on neutral ground and talk. Would that work for you?"

"Yeah, that would work. Do you want us to come now?"

"If you're available, yes. Or I can stop by your home later."

"Now is fine. Where are you located?"

She gave me the address, and I was familiar with the area.

"We'll be there in about twenty minutes."

"Perfect. I'll see you then."

I hung up, and my eyes shifted to the rearview mirror again. "Hey, buddy," I said to Noah, "we're going to make a quick stop before we get something to eat, okay?"

"Okay." He never looked up.

When we arrived at the building where the Safe Harbor Child Advocacy office was located, I parked my vehicle, climbed out, and helped Noah down from the backseat. I held his smaller hand in mine as we walked toward the building. When we were almost at the door, I saw a petite woman standing out front. She couldn't be more than five foot three, with dark brown skin and her natural hair parted in the middle and smoothed into a bun at her nape. In tan slacks and a cream blouse, she appeared professional yet approachable.

She smiled and extended her hand. "Marcus?"

"That's me." I took her smaller hand in mine and briefly shook it. Oddly, I experienced a tingling sensation in the palm of my hand but ignored it. Granted, I found her attractive, but this was not the time to get distracted.

"I'm Julia. Nice to meet you."

"Likewise. This little guy right here is Noah." I made my voice sound more animated to try to get a response out of him, but he kept looking down at the pavement.

Julia crouched to his level and softened her voice. "Hi, Noah. I'm Miss Julia. I love your costume. Are you Robin, Batman's sidekick?"

He nodded, not meeting her eyes.

"I always liked Robin. He's very brave, just like Batman."

He didn't acknowledge her comment at all this time.

Julia stood. "Let's go over to the park."

We crossed the street, and she asked Noah if he'd like to get on the swing.

"Okay," he said, his answer to everything in the same lifeless voice.

A little girl who appeared a few years older than him was on one of the swings. She looked at him with curiosity as he sat down. He held on to the metal chains on either side of the seat and just sat there, barely moving.

"How's he doing?" Julia asked in a low voice.

"Not great," I admitted. "He's not eating and doesn't speak unless spoken to. This is a kid who used to talk my ear off every time I went over to his house. Now... nothing. And he refuses to take off the costume. He wears it all day and only changes when it's time to go to bed and put on his pajamas."

"For a child who has experienced his type of trauma, the costume probably has some special meaning. It's providing comfort and makes him feel safe and powerful, offering a little bit of control in a world that for him has careened out of control and become unfamiliar without his parents."

I watched his bent head, and my chest burned with sorrow. "What should I do?"

"Let him keep the security of the costume for now. He

needs it. Keep it washed and clean, and let's see how long this period continues. You said he isn't eating. Has he shown interest in *any* food you've offered?"

"Nothing. Not pizza, not cereal, not chicken nuggets. What kid doesn't like chicken nuggets? I know I've seen him eat them, but he isn't interested in anything children normally like. I called his babysitter, and she gave me suggestions, but the result is the same. He barely acknowledges the plates I put in front of him."

Julia was quiet for a moment, which gave me an opportunity to study her. Her skin wasn't simply dark brown. It was a deep, even brown that glowed like burnished bronze. She had high cheekbones and a graceful nose that flowed into full, sculpted lips. I couldn't tell the length of her natural hair, but the style flattered the symmetry of her features and exposed the enticingly feminine slope of her neck.

I briefly looked at her hands. No ring. Surprising. But a woman who looked like her probably had a man. She had an open, friendly face and was attractive in a girl-next-door kind of way.

She swung her head in my direction, and when our eyes met, my breath caught. I'd lost track of the many women I'd slept with over the years. I liked women, period. So I never considered myself as having a type, but if I did, it would be this woman right here. Whoever her man was—if she had one—he was a lucky bastard.

"What does Noah call you?" Julia asked.

"He calls me Uncle Marcus. He's been doing that since he was a toddler," I answered.

"Mind if I talk to him alone for a minute?"

"Go right ahead," I said, though I doubted she would make any progress.

She walked away, the skinny heels of her shoes sinking into

the grass with each step, her hips swinging gently from left to right as she moved. There was something about Julia that captured my attention.

If we had met under different circumstances, I'd definitely holler at her.

Chapter 3

Julia

I approached the little boy, who was sitting practically motionless on the swing. When I stopped in front of him, he didn't lift his eyes.

I lowered myself to his level again and smiled, though he wasn't looking at me. "Hi, Noah."

"Hi."

The girl beside him jumped off her swing and ran toward a group of other kids.

"Your Uncle Marcus told me that you haven't been eating very much. Is that true?" I kept my voice light because I didn't want him to feel as if he was being chastised.

He remained silent.

"I know you've been going through a very rough time, and I'm here to help. One of the things I want to do is help you find something to eat. It's very important that you eat and drink so you can grow up big and strong like Robin."

Still nothing.

"If you don't like the food that your Uncle Marcus offers you, what would you like to eat?"

"Nothing."

Progress. He had actually answered a question.

"Oh, I doubt that. There must be something you like. It can be anything you want."

I waited, and after almost a minute, he said in a small voice, "Ice cream."

"Ice cream. I like ice cream too. Do you want any particular flavor?"

He shrugged.

"I have an idea. Why don't we tell your Uncle Marcus that you want to have some ice cream? The good news is, there's an ice cream truck right here in the park, and you can have some right now."

He lifted his gaze, and my heart cracked a little at the sadness in his eyes. But I saw a little hope too.

Without saying a word, I stood and extended my hand to him. He took it, and we walked over to Marcus.

"Noah," I said gently, "can you tell Uncle Marcus what you told me you'd like to eat?"

He stared at his own feet. "Ice cream."

Marcus stared blankly at me. "Ice cream?"

"I told him he could have anything he wanted, and that's what he said," I explained. "There's an ice cream truck on the other side of the park. They're here every afternoon to capitalize on all the kids and parents hanging out after school."

Marcus looked at his godson. "If that's what he wants, that's what he'll get."

Marcus Hayes was wearing a light blue dress shirt, tie, and slacks. No ring, which meant he was a man taking on the responsibility of a child on his own—essentially becoming a single dad.

His face was vaguely familiar, but I couldn't figure out why. Had we met before? If we had, I felt as if I would have remembered meeting such a striking man. He was a couple of inches over six feet, with golden brown skin and a neat, trim beard that framed thick, juicy-looking lips. As we strolled through the park, I noticed how the eyes of several women followed him when we walked past. I understood, but I also couldn't let his appearance influence my assessment of him.

Noah held onto my hand the entire time until we arrived at Something Sweet, a purple truck with its name written in cheerful yellow and orange letters on the side. There were a few people ahead of us, so we waited in line until it was our turn.

Once we arrived at the window, a twenty-something woman with curly brown hair greeted us with a smile. "What can I get for you folks?"

"I'll take a vanilla ice cream. What about you, Marcus?"

He seemed bewildered by the question. I could tell he hadn't intended to eat any ice cream, but I sent him a message with my eyes. *Follow my lead. This is for Noah.* Fortunately, he understood.

"Coffee flavor for me," he said.

"And you, Noah?" I asked.

He finally lifted his head. "I don't know." His voice shook.

"What flavors do you have?" I asked the vendor.

She went through a short list, and when she finished, I looked down at the little boy. "Chocolate sounds pretty good," I said.

He nodded. "Chocolate."

"That's one vanilla, one coffee, and one chocolate, coming right up," the woman said in a cheery voice. "Cones?"

I glanced at Marcus, and he nodded.

"Yes," I replied.

The first person to receive their ice cream was Noah. He held the cone with both hands and immediately began eating.

Not licking, not a tentative bite, but a real bite, as if he would devour the ice cream right away.

"Good?" I asked as I took my cone.

He nodded, focused on the ice cream.

Marcus paid, and the three of us started walking in the direction we'd come from. Back at the same location, Marcus and I sat down on a bench next to each other, but Noah continued standing, clearly enjoying his treat.

"This is the most I've seen him eat in four days," Marcus said in a low voice, staring in amazement.

"You just needed to find the right thing. Ice cream isn't exactly nutritious, but it's a start to get him eating again."

When Noah finished the ice cream, he licked his sticky fingers and then went back over to the swing. He sat down, and this time he rocked a little more than before as he watched the other kids play on the slides and the merry-go-round.

"While he's busy, time for a candid conversation. How are you handling all of this?" I asked.

Marcus laughed, which softened his features, wiping away the somber expression that had dominated his face since we met. My heart did an odd little flip-flop. Okay, he was attractive and definitely my type, but this was not the time to become distracted by a fine man. He was grieving the death of his best friend, and his "child" was technically a client. Crossing that line would be tacky at best, unethical at worst.

"Real talk? I feel like I'm drowning. I have no idea what I'm doing, and I've had to cut back my hours because I'm so concerned about him. Luckily, I have three great assistants and the kind of job where I can do some work from home, but I've had to get some of my fellow real estate agents to help me with some of the work so that I don't completely blow off my clients. I don't know what he needs or how to talk to him."

A real estate agent. I'd probably seen his face on a billboard or sign, which was why he looked familiar.

I heard the frustration in his voice, but I also heard that he wanted to do better. "You're here. You're present. That counts for a lot. What's going on with his aunt in Tennessee? Will she be coming to pick him up?"

He frowned for a moment. "She and I talked the other night. She's Brandon's sister, and she has kids and a husband and a stable home. She definitely wants him."

I sensed hesitation. "But?" I prompted.

He shrugged. "I'm not ready to ship him off yet. I want to make sure he's mentally in a good place. That's my responsibility right now, and I don't think he needs more disruptions at the moment."

"I have a list of therapists that I can recommend. Talking to a professional might do him some good."

"Yeah, I'd like that."

"When I get back to my office, I'll text you the names. What about you? Do you need someone to talk to, to help you until Noah's aunt takes over? I have a list of guardian support groups I could recommend."

He shook his head. "No, I'm good."

"If you change your mind, let me know. As for Noah, if you need help narrowing down the list, I can help. That's what I'm here for—to help. You don't have to bear this burden alone. If you let me know which school he attends, I'll talk to the administration and offer guidance on how to handle Noah when he returns to school."

"That would be very helpful. I really appreciate what you've done so far. The ice cream idea... I would've never thought of that."

I smiled. "I didn't actually come up with it on my own. I let him tell me what he wanted. As adults, we often think we know what's best, and we base our decisions on those thoughts. But children will also let us know what's in their best interest. What makes them happy. What makes them comfortable."

"Like the Robin costume," he said.

"Exactly. Give him time, and go easy on yourself. Taking care of a child is a huge responsibility, and you're doing much better than you think. Noah is lucky to have you."

He looked doubtful but also appreciative of the compliment. It was clear he needed reassurance, to know he wasn't completely screwing up.

"I'm going to head back to the office. It was really nice to meet you and see you. I'll check in again in a few more days to see how the two of you are doing." I stood.

Marcus stood too. "How long do you typically work with clients?"

"It depends on the case and the end goal. If I'm offering short-term crisis support, my assistance is only required for a few months. If a child is in a high-risk environment, I monitor the situation for a year or longer. In your case, the goal is to finalize guardianship, which shouldn't take long since Noah has an aunt willing to take him." I turned my attention to the little boy. "Noah, I'm going back to work. It was nice to meet you."

He jumped off the swing and stood beside it, his expression uncertain. Then he slowly walked over to the two of us. "You're leaving?"

I nodded. "I have to go back to work, but I'll be in touch in a few days to check in on you and Uncle Marcus."

"I liked the ice cream," he said.

"I'm glad to hear that. But if you want to grow up big and strong like Robin, you can't only eat ice cream. You have to eat some of the other food Uncle Marcus puts on your plate too. Will you try?"

He nodded.

"Good."

The three of us walked out of the park and crossed the street. We said goodbye at the door of my building, but I didn't go inside. I stood on the sidewalk, eyes glued to the two of them. As I watched, Noah reached for Marcus's hand.

They stopped at the blue SUV they had pulled up in, which I now noticed had a vanity plate—Romeo, with an Alpha Phi Alpha frame. *Oh boy*. Probably a player. None of my business, though.

I went into the building so Marcus wouldn't catch me staring and climbed the stairs to the second floor. I needed to start on my report and forward those resources I promised him.

My assessment so far: though it would take time, my gut told me those two would be just fine.

Chapter 4

Julia

I walked along the carpeted hallway on the way to my apartment while fishing the keys out of my purse. I'd had a long day, but as I neared the door, I heard a sound that had become pleasantly commonplace over the past few weeks —the muffled sound of children's laughter.

I pushed open the door and had barely crossed the threshold when I heard, "Aunt Julia!"

My three-year-old goddaughter, Emma, slammed into me and wrapped her arms around my legs with enthusiasm. And just like that, the stress and frustrations of the day melted away.

I dropped my purse on the entryway table and scooped her up in one fluid motion. "Hey there! Did you have a good day?" I tweaked her nose.

She giggled, her dark curls bouncing as she nodded her head vigorously. "We made cookies!" she exclaimed, her blue eyes brightening with the memory.

I gasped in mock shock, pressing my hand to my chest. "You made cookies without me? I'm devastated."

"We saved you some," Emma assured me with the earnest innocence of a toddler.

Leanne, my best friend and current roommate, appeared from the direction of the kitchen, wiping her hands on a dish towel. Average height and slender, she wore her blonde hair pulled into a bun on top of her head.

"I barely managed to save you any because she ate *seven of them*," Leanne said, staring at her daughter.

Emma buried her face in my shoulder.

"I don't believe a word you said." I kissed the top of her head, and Leanne rolled her eyes and headed back into the kitchen.

"Did you have a good day at work?" Emma asked.

"I sure did," I replied, settling her on my hip. "Did you have a good day at home?"

"Mhmm. Mommy said I could have one more cookie for dessert after dinner." She held her forefinger in front of my face to emphasize the point.

"Good plan. We can eat our cookies together."

Her face brightened. "Okay."

She kicked her feet, a signal that she wanted me to put her down. As she scampered toward the living room, I followed my nose to the kitchen, where the aroma of some unknown pasta dish beckoned to me.

The kitchen wasn't very big, but it was functional. A small table sat in front of two small windows that overlooked the front of the building and the street below. Three stools sat in front of the bar, adding more seating and offering a view of the rest of the space, which included black appliances and enough counter space to hold small appliances like the microwave and air fryer.

As I sat on one of the stools, Leanne poured a glass of white wine and set it in front of me.

"Marry me," I said as I gratefully clasped the stem.

She laughed. "Sorry, honey, I'm already married."

I tipped back my head and drank half the wine.

Her left eyebrow lifted higher. "Rough day?"

I set down the glass and sighed. "You have no idea."

She and I had been best friends since we were passing notes in English class at twelve years old. We went to different colleges after high school—she studied in California while I stayed in Texas—but we remained best friends throughout those four years.

I was the maid of honor at her wedding and godmother to her two kids. Our closeness meant that when she separated from her husband, Owen, I was the one she called. Not her judgmental family who insisted she try to work things out or any of her other friends—me, the one person she said she could always count on. So for the past few weeks, here we were, two women and two little girls, crammed into a one-bedroom apartment. At night, they slept on my sleeper sofa, and each day Leanne hoped her husband would come to his senses and demand she return home.

Unfortunately for her, that hadn't happened yet.

"Want to talk about your day?" she asked.

"Aunt Julia!"

Leanne's six-year-old daughter, Paige, came rushing into the kitchen. Like her sister, she had a head full of dark curls and blue eyes.

"Look." She proudly held up a sheet of white paper with a drawing on it.

"*Wow*. That's... something," I said, not really sure what I was looking at. I shot my friend a look, hoping for a hint, but all she did was shrug. Apparently, she had no idea what Paige had drawn, either.

"Do you know what it is?" Paige asked.

I was afraid she'd test me, which was why I'd sought assistance from her mother. "Is it..."

I tilted my head, studying the image. I was pretty sure I saw four legs, and maybe ears. Or were they horns?

"Is it a horse?"

"No!" Paige giggled.

I tapped my chin. "Oh, I see. It's a dog, isn't it?"

"No!" She dissolved into laughter, shaking her head so hard that her curls whipped across her face. "It's a cow!"

I smacked my forehead dramatically. "Of course! I see it now."

I glanced at Leanne, who was biting her bottom lip to keep from laughing out loud. I shot her a dirty look.

Paige swung toward her mother. "Mommy, can we put it on the fridge?"

"Of course, baby. Let me get some tape."

Leanne pulled tape from the junk drawer and affixed the drawing to the right door of the refrigerator, below Paige's other drawing that was allegedly a picture of her and her sister playing with a puppy.

"Thank you, Mommy." Paige beamed with pride.

"You're welcome. Good job!" Leanne gave her daughter a high-five, and Paige pranced out of the room.

"You're so fake," I told my friend.

"Oh look, the pot is calling the kettle black." She pulled on oven mitts. "You were going to tell me about your day before Paige came in."

Though space was limited in my apartment because she and her daughters were staying here, I didn't mind. I had lived by myself for a long time and always assumed I was a loner, but I enjoyed the company. As a plus, every day I came home from work, Leanne had dinner ready or almost ready. I was getting spoiled and would miss her and the girls when she and Owen reconciled.

"It was one of those days," I said, watching as she pulled a bubbling baked ziti out of the oven. "I won't bore you with the details, but I had two court appearances today—one was a child custody case, and the other was to testify about an interview I had with a nine-year-old who was being abused by a parent."

Leanne grimaced. "I know that was hard to deal with."

"It was," I admitted. "Then in the afternoon, I got called to the ER. I have a new case involving a toddler with suspicious injuries."

"Darn it, Jules. How could people hurt kids?"

"I'll never understand it for as long as I live." I took a sip of wine. "The day wasn't all bad. I saw one of my new clients today—a little boy who lost his parents in a car accident. This will be an easy one, mostly paperwork. His godfather is his temporary guardian. They came by the office, and the boy wasn't talking or eating, but I got him to eat some ice cream, and he seemed in slightly better spirits when he left."

"That's good news. Poor kid. He must be so traumatized."

"He is, and his guardian seems a little out of his depth, but he's trying, and that's what's important."

"We're all trying," Leanne said, pouring herself a glass of wine. "I'm not surprised the little boy was better after spending time with you. You were born for this work. You're so good with kids. I know you've heard me say this before, but you'd make a great mom. You should reconsider having children."

"Bite your tongue."

"Oh come on, being a parent is not that bad. You're practically doing the work now with all your cases. You need one or two of your own." A mischievous glint appeared in her eyes.

Holding up my hands, I crossed my fingers, as if warding off a vampire.

"Would you stop!" She slapped my hands down. "I'm being serious. You're a natural."

"It's one thing to be fun Aunt Julia or Ms. Richmond, the child advocate. Motherhood is completely different and is too much responsibility. I like kids. I love *your* kids, but I want zero, zed, nada—none of my own. The stress would probably kill me. Now, enough about me." I dropped my voice. "Have you heard from Owen?"

Her smile faltered, and I immediately regretted bringing him up.

She stared into her glass of wine. "He texted this morning and asked how the girls are doing. He didn't ask about *me*. Just the girls."

"You know that doesn't mean anything, right? Most men are idiots."

She sighed. "I love him, Jules. Really, I do, but I'm not going to be invisible in my own marriage and taken for granted. I'm a person, not just someone who manages the house and keeps the kids fed. I have a degree—one I set aside to be a wife and mother, and instead of showing his appreciation, he acts as if he's entitled to my time and labor. He got comfortable. Complacent. At least, that's what I thought. What if he doesn't miss me? What if he's glad I'm gone?" Her voice shook.

"Of course he misses you. You and the girls," I said.

"I'm not so sure. I left three weeks ago, and he hasn't asked me to come home."

I stretched across the counter and opened my hands. She placed her hands in mine.

Squeezing her fingers reassuringly, I asked, "Do you regret leaving?"

"No, but..." She sighed.

"He'll come around once he realizes what he'll lose if you don't go home."

"I hope you're right."

"When am I ever wrong?"

We both laughed.

Leanne withdrew her hands. "I hope you're hungry. I have to prepare the salad, and then dinner will be ready."

"Eat without me. I'm not very hungry."

"Are you sure?"

"I'm sure. I'll fix a plate when I'm ready. In the meantime, I'm getting out of these clothes." I didn't have much of an appetite after the cases I'd dealt with today. And I was tired.

When I closed the door of my bedroom, it was like sealing myself into a vault. With more people in the apartment, my bedroom had become a sanctuary of pastel colors—mostly pink, lilac, and powder blue.

I kicked off my shoes and stripped out of my skirt and blouse, tossing them to the floor. Strolling across the carpet to the window, I looked out at Houston's sprawling nightscape, which was alive with lights.

Somewhere out there was little Noah in his Robin costume and his godfather. "Uncle Marcus," I whispered. Player or not, I couldn't stop thinking about him.

They had been the bright spot in a rough day. I recalled their walk to the SUV and the way Noah had reached for his godfather's hand. Some clients stuck with me, and they certainly did.

I hoped they were doing okay.

Chapter 5

Marcus

"Noah! Come on, buddy, let's go!" I hollered, glancing at the clock on the microwave.

I was running around like a chicken with its head cut off. When the alarm went off this morning, I had bolted upright in bed, unaccustomed to getting up so early. But today was Noah's first day back at school. He'd had two sessions with one of the therapists Julia recommended, and the therapist had cleared him to return, but he was scheduled to continue seeing her twice a week.

My phone buzzed on the counter. Another text from Brandon's sister, Zenobia: *Have you thought about what we discussed?*

Jaw tight, I stared at the message. We'd talked at the funeral and twice since then. I told her it was best for Noah to finish school here. He only had about six weeks left. What was the point of uprooting him and causing more upheaval in his life? She insisted he should move to Tennessee right away and explained she and her husband had two kids of their own and a nice house on an acre near Nashville.

"Noah should be with family. Real family."

Maybe I wasn't his *real* family, and maybe I was just a thirty-three-year-old bachelor who could have gone his whole life without having kids and been perfectly happy. But I didn't believe it was a good idea to send Noah to Tennessee right now. I definitely didn't feel like having a text argument with her this early in the morning while I was trying to get him ready for his first day back.

Two Pop-Tarts shot up in the toaster, and I dropped them onto a plate. These and fries were the only things my godson was eating. He had apparently lost interest in ice cream because he hadn't eaten a bite of the cartons of vanilla and chocolate that were sitting in the freezer.

I poured orange juice into a cup. "Noah—"

The sentence died in my throat when he walked into the kitchen, fully dressed like Robin again. My heart sank because I didn't want to disappoint him.

"Hey, buddy," I said carefully. "Did you need me to help you get dressed?"

"I'm already dressed." His solemn brown eyes looked directly into mine.

I took a breath, racking my brain, wondering what was the right thing to say. "You can't wear the costume to school. Remember, I explained that to you last night."

I had laid out khaki pants and a green shirt, but when I tried to help him get dressed, he had told me he could dress himself. Now I knew why.

"I want to." He spoke in a quiet but firm voice, his chin jutting in defiance.

I moved closer and dropped to his eye level, the way I had seen Julia do. "I know you do, but the school has rules. You have to wear regular clothes."

"I want to wear this."

"Noah—"

"I have to, Uncle Marcus." His voice cracked, and the fingers of his right hand bunched in the cape.

"Why do you have to?" I asked gently.

Unshed tears shimmered in his eyes, and I felt like shit.

"Noah, I know you're upset, but—"

"I *have* to!" he shouted, tears spilling down his cheeks. "Daddy said I could—" His voice broke completely, and he dissolved into sobs, his small body shaking as tears poured over the mask and streamed down his chin.

I pulled him into my arms. "It's okay, buddy. You can wear it."

I held him until he eased out of my arms. Looking at me with red-rimmed eyes, he asked, "Can I really?"

"For as long as you want."

Maybe that was the wrong call. I don't know. I didn't know what the hell I was doing, but I couldn't stand to see him cry.

I lifted off the mask and wiped away his tears. "If I let you wear the costume, you have to do something for me. I need you to eat something and drink some juice. Can you do that for me?"

He seemed to consider the question, and then he nodded.

"More than one bite," I said.

He nodded again.

Relieved, I smiled. "Good."

The rest of the morning was less eventful as I grabbed my traveling mug of coffee that said *Houston's #1 Realtor*—a gift from Brandon. He'd given it to me as a joke three years ago. I tried not to think about the fact that I'd never receive another gag gift from him again.

I picked up my satchel and guided Noah out the door with his breakfast in hand.

Almost twenty minutes later, I pulled onto the school

grounds and parked. Noah sat in the backseat with a half-eaten Pop-Tart and an empty kids' travel tumbler.

"Ready to go inside?" I asked, eyeing him in the rearview mirror. He'd put the mask back on.

He nodded.

We walked across the parking lot, me holding his hand, his backpack in my other hand, and his cape fluttering behind him like a real superhero on a mission.

His teacher, Mrs. Hinds, was waiting at the classroom door—an older Black woman with kind eyes and graying black hair. A warm smile touched her lips when she saw us.

"Hello, Noah!" she said with enthusiasm. "Welcome back. We've missed you."

He responded by gripping my hand tighter.

"I love your Robin costume," she added.

I cleared my throat. "Mind if I speak to you for a quick minute?" I asked.

"Certainly." She gestured to her assistant, who came to the door and extended a hand to Noah.

He looked up at me.

"It's okay," I assured him.

He went to her, looking back once before allowing her to lead him to his desk.

I turned to Mrs. Hinds. "I'm sorry about the costume. I tried to get him to change, but he got really upset. I was told not to push him to wear anything else, that the suit probably provides comfort because of what happened."

Her expression softened. "It's perfectly fine and not uncommon. We've had children arrive at school dressed as princesses, ballerinas, in their pajamas—believe me, it's not a problem. If this helps him feel safe and comfortable, we can accommodate him."

"Glad to hear that."

"The counselor spoke with the teaching staff about what happened. She spoke to Ms. Richmond, the child advocate. We're well aware of what he's been through and are here to support you and him."

Tension drained from my body at her words. Julia had kept her word and had been working behind the scenes. She had done another check-in last week, but our conversation had been brief.

"That means a lot. I just want to make sure he's okay."

"Don't you worry. We'll keep an eye on him and call you if there are any problems." She briefly touched my arm. "Don't fret too much. Pick your battles. And FYI, kids are awfully resilient. Give him time."

Her reassurance was exactly what I needed since I was doubting myself. In some ways, I felt like I was drowning in a whirlpool and he was being sucked down with me.

"One more thing you should know. He hasn't been eating much, so he might not eat lunch."

"Ms. Richmond informed the counselor of the issue. Grief can affect the appetite of adults, so I'm not surprised. The counselor had some suggestions, so I'll try to get him to eat something."

"Thanks."

Before I left, I peeked through the window in the door. Noah sat at his desk with his cape draped over the back of the chair, staring straight ahead.

I didn't want to leave him, but I had to go to work. I hoped he'd be okay. For the past two weeks, I'd felt as if a heavy stone was in the pit of my stomach, and the sensation hadn't lessened. How did people do this? I was stressed the hell out, and I'd only been a parent for two weeks.

In the car, my phone buzzed, this time alerting me to an email in my inbox. I checked the message and discovered the insurance company was requesting yet another piece of documentation. Brandon had been paying on a million-dollar life insurance policy, with his wife and son as the beneficiaries. Since Stacey passed with him, the entire amount was due to Noah.

I forwarded the email to the estate attorney and included a brief message explaining I'd look for the paperwork this evening. Then I took off for the office.

Overnight, my life had gone through a seismic shift. I was responsible for another human being who barely spoke, barely ate, and whose eyes were filled with more sadness than any kid should have to endure. At the same time, I had to keep working. I had three showings today, emails to respond to, and I had to check on a couple of my listings. It was early yet, but soon my phone would be buzzing with calls and texts from clients and colleagues.

I parked my SUV at the back of Houston Realty, a one-story brick building near the center of town. I'd been here ever since I earned my license. Before I got out, I glanced in the back seat and saw the abandoned Pop-Tart and empty juice cup and shook my head. He'd finished the juice, but he still hadn't eaten much. He'd barely eaten anything in the past two weeks—except for the ice cream he gobbled up at the park with Julia.

Julia Richmond with the hip-swinging walk, friendly personality, and the ability to break through the wall Noah had erected. For a brief moment at the park, I saw the old Noah trying to emerge. The one I used to ruthlessly tickle, wrestle with, and chase around the house—much to the chagrin of his mother, Stacey.

"Take it outside!" she used to yell.

I smiled to myself. Man, what I wouldn't give to hear her pissed-off voice again.

Didn't Julia say the truck was usually at the park in the

afternoons? If ice cream was the one food Noah was willing to eat, the one food that made him become a semblance of his old self, then that's what he was going to get.

Pick your battles, Mrs. Hinds had said.

You know what, ice cream wasn't all bad. One of the main ingredients was milk, and milk was good for growing kids.

I walked to the door with renewed vigor. I was taking Noah for ice cream again, and it wouldn't hurt to put in a call to Julia to let her know how he was doing and that we were stopping by.

Chapter 6

Marcus

Two weeks ago, I pulled up near this park and bought ice cream for Noah. Now I was back, scanning the park as we crossed the street, surprisingly anxious to see Julia, who said she would meet us at the truck.

I helped Noah down from the car, and he adjusted his cape so it hung properly, the mask still covering his eyes. Robin was once again on a mission to save the day. Or eat ice cream, whichever was more pressing.

He and I entered the park, sidestepping a woman pushing a stroller while holding a baby in her arms. Like before, there were kids playing on the slide, swings, and merry-go-round, screaming, laughing, and yelling the way kids do, enjoying themselves.

My sidekick and I bypassed all of them and made a beeline for the purple truck. When I had picked Noah up from school and told him where we were going, he had asked, "Are we going to get ice cream?" His voice had carried the faintest hint of interest.

When I confirmed that's what we were going to do, he sat forward in his seat and asked, "Will Miss Julia be there?"

More than interest in his voice then. I had heard the faint sound of hope, and with great pleasure, I told him she would be there because I'd already confirmed with her. He sat back without a word and folded his arms with a certain satisfaction that couldn't be denied.

As we walked through the park, I smoothed down my shirt and straightened my jacket, which was ridiculous because I was there for Noah to have ice cream, not to impress his child advocate.

As we drew nearer to the truck, I saw her. This time she was wearing gray slacks and a white shirt, and heels again. Her hair was in the same conservative style, her dark brown skin seeming to glow in the afternoon sunlight as she watched us approach.

When I pledged Alpha Phi Alpha back in college, I had been given the name Romeo, a name I'd had since high school that started as a joke. I had a reputation for knowing when a woman was interested and the ability to read subtle signals that a lot of guys missed. I used those skills to charm my way into women's panties. So as we approached Julia, I put my skills to use, catching the way her eyes flickered to mine and held for a beat too long. I noticed the slight straightening in her posture and how her smile shifted from friendly to something warmer, more intimate.

She was definitely interested. I wasn't misreading the signals.

And me, I was interested too. I had thought about her a lot since the last time we spoke, and seeing her again elevated my heart rate.

She dropped her gaze to Noah. "Look at you! Hi, Robin. What's your other name again? Boy something."

"Boy Wonder," he answered.

Wow, that was better than last time when he had barely spoken until it was time to order his frozen treat.

She snapped her fingers. "That's right, Boy Wonder," she said, as if he had shared the most fascinating nugget of information. "So, what flavor of ice cream is the Boy Wonder going to have today? Chocolate again?"

Noah shook his head, the slightest smile on his lips. "Vanilla."

"That's my personal favorite. It's a classic flavor. Good choice." She finally lifted her gaze to me, and I felt the full force of her brown eyes, my stomach contracting as my attraction to her intensified ten-fold. "What are you having today?" she asked.

I'd like to have you. The thought startled me, but fortunately, I caught myself before I said the sexually suggestive words out loud.

"Coffee, no ice cream. And yourself?"

"I think I'll try strawberry today. I'm treating this time."

I shook my head. "Absolutely not. I've got this."

"You don't have to—"

"It's the least I can do for you being so helpful."

"I'm doing my job," she said.

"I'm pretty sure your job doesn't include buying ice cream for your client and his guardian."

We placed our orders with the vendor, and after she handed over the cones and my cup of coffee, we all walked away. Noah ate his ice cream with even more enthusiasm than the first time.

"So, Robin," Julia said, "What's the best part of being a superhero?"

He seemed to seriously consider the answer, as if he really were a superhero. It was hard not to laugh, but I didn't want to disrupt this moment. Once again, she was making progress with him.

"You can help people," Noah answered.

"That's a really good answer. Do you like helping people?"

Clutching the cone in his hand, he nodded.

Her eyes met mine above his head, and a certain recognition manifested between us. Not wholly related to Noah, but to us too. Awareness hummed in the air—the knowledge men and women have had of each other since the beginning of time. Much as we might try to ignore it, it couldn't be denied. Not when there was mutual attraction, and that was certainly the case here.

We sat down on one of the benches, and Noah sat between us, licking his ice cream with single-minded focus. There was a stark difference between how he behaved here, eating ice cream, and his sadness at the condo, pushing around the dinner I attempted to feed him.

He was more upbeat in Julia's presence. More lively. The vanilla dessert dripped down the cone and onto his fingers, but he didn't care. He licked it off and then kept going.

"All gone," he finally announced proudly. Both the ice cream and the cone had vanished.

Julia was still working on hers. She took her time. She was careful. Deliberate. A bead of melted strawberry slid toward her thumb, and her pink tongue flicked out, slow and precise, tracing the curve before it could fall. She circled the top again, smoothing the edges. Completely in control.

Goddamn.

I swallowed.

Her actions shouldn't have affected me. It was ice cream. In broad daylight. At a crowded park. But I was mesmerized.

I tracked the movement of her mouth, the way her full lips pressed against the cone, and the quiet concentration in her expression. There was something intimate about the way she tasted it, unhurried, unaware of the effect she was having. My crotch tightened, and I shifted on the bench, dragging my gaze away before she caught me staring.

"Was it good?" I asked Noah.

"Delicious," he said in his solemn voice.

"Your Uncle Marcus told me you went to school today. Did you have fun?" Julia asked.

Noah nodded.

"What was fun?"

He told her about what he did at school, going into much more detail than when I'd asked him how his day went.

"For doing a good job, I got to go to the Reading Corner. We have bean bag chairs and mats on the floor," he explained.

"Ooh, I love bean bag chairs. They're soft and squishy."

Noah smiled, such a rare occurrence that I had to stare. The woman was a miracle worker.

"Soft and squishy," he repeated, almost shyly.

Julia grinned at him. "Which book did you read?"

He squinted, trying to remember. "There was a cat on the front. I don't remember the name."

"That's okay. Did you enjoy the story?" She was really good at drawing him out by asking questions, giving a master class on how to make someone feel seen.

"Yes. I like cats. Mommy and Daddy said I can have one when I'm older." A flicker of sadness crossed his face, and his voice lowered. "But they..."

Panic rose inside me. I wanted to scoop him up and protect him from the painful thoughts.

"You miss them." Julia spoke in a soft voice. She didn't panic. She was calm.

"Yeah." His shoulders slumped.

"That makes sense," Julia continued gently. "When a

memory of your mom and dad comes up, missing them can feel really big."

"Yeah," he said again, his voice lower and thicker.

A small pause.

"It's still okay to like cats," Julia said. "And it's okay to miss your mom and dad."

Noah looked up at her. "Mommy liked cats too. She had a cat when she was little, and his name was Brutus."

"Brutus. What a cool name."

He smiled faintly. "When I have a cat, I'm going to name him Brutus too."

"Just like your mommy's?"

He sat up taller. "Yeah," he said with conviction.

"I think that's a great idea." Julia had somehow navigated a painful conversation with ease.

Noah looked up at me. "Can I go on the swings?"

"Sure," I answered.

He jumped up with more energy than I'd seen in a long time and rushed over to the swings, his cape flying behind him. I watched him with a mix of sadness and relief. I was sad he had experienced loss at such a young age and wasn't himself at the moment, but relieved that I was starting to see his personality shine through.

"How did you do that?" I asked.

She understood the question right away. "All I did was validate his pain and put a name to what he was feeling. There's no quick fix for what he's going through, but we can help him navigate this period. Did you read the materials I emailed you?"

"I did, but I blanked in the moment."

"I've had years of practice," she said, her voice kind. "How has your day been?"

I relaxed, reaching my hand across the back of the bench, an inch or two from her shoulder. "Surprisingly good. Work went well, and I was able to catch up on a few tasks. Considering this was Noah's first day back at school, I was a little worried, but everything seemed to go well. Better than expected. His teacher didn't have a problem with him wearing the costume, so that was definitely a win."

"You have to pick your battles with kids," Julia said, speaking with understanding instead of judgment.

"So I've heard."

We sat there talking for a little longer while Noah swung back and forth, and I nursed my coffee. Julia finished her dessert and listened as I gave an update on his therapy sessions.

I didn't want to leave, but we had to, and I was sure Julia needed to get back to work. I stood and called out to Noah.

He hopped off the swing and came running over. *Running.* That was new too.

"Thanks for... everything," I said to Julia. I wasn't just thanking her for meeting us for ice cream. I appreciated her talking to him and making him smile.

We headed back across the street and stood in the doorway of her building.

Her gaze held mine. "It's always nice to see the two of you," she said politely. She turned her attention to the superhero beside me. "Keep up the good work at school, okay?"

"Okay," Noah promised.

"Bye," I said.

"Bye."

I didn't move, and neither did she. Then we both laughed a little awkwardly.

"Take care. Come on, buddy," I said.

"Bye! See you tomorrow." Noah waved as we walked away.

I pulled up short.

Julia laughed, surprised. Then she waited, a question in her eyes.

"I guess we'll be back tomorrow," I said.

Her smile was soft and genuine. "I'll be here. Same time?"

"Same time," I confirmed.

Noah and I headed to my vehicle. He was quiet, but he had more bounce in his step and was no longer walking with his head down. I loved seeing the difference in him. It gave me hope.

As I pulled away from the curb, I checked the rearview mirror. Julia hadn't gone inside yet. She was on the sidewalk, talking to a young couple. Maybe they were the parents of clients who had stopped by, like we had.

Looking at Noah in the backseat, his body relaxed and his face less solemn, I wondered if she had any idea how much she had transformed him.

Later, I'd have to deal with the stresses of life: responding to Zenobia's text, which I had ignored all day. I'd have to find the documentation for the insurance company. I'd have to figure out how to preserve some of this lightness of being Noah was experiencing.

But come tomorrow, I could relax again, because we'd come back here. To Something Sweet.

To her.

Chapter 7

Julia

"Going for ice cream again?"

My co-worker's question stopped me on the way to the stairs. She eyed me over her black frames, her dark hair piled on top of her head in a messy updo.

Gina was observant. Too observant.

"It's so good, you know?"

I was doing too much. I knew it. There was no need for me to spend so much time on this case, and I didn't need to see them yet again. Marcus could provide updates over the phone, but I couldn't help myself. Nor could I stop the familiar tingle in my chest each time they arrived. Little Noah and his Uncle Marcus had captured my... not *heart.* My *attention.*

"Want me to bring you back an ice cream?" I asked, knowing full well she was severely lactose intolerant.

"I can't, but thanks for asking."

"Sure."

I carefully descended the stairs, today wearing heels and a figure-hugging taupe dress that clung to my derriere enough to show it off without being improper. I had no business dressing like this, but a part of me wanted Marcus to notice. I was fairly certain he was already interested, but I couldn't be sure.

I shouldn't care. Any man with *Romeo* on his license plate should be kept at a distance, but it wasn't my fault I was developing a crush. Did he need to come for ice cream every day this week? Probably not. But I was glad he did, and I suspected he didn't mind Noah's addiction to the dessert, either.

I was out the door and standing in front of the building approximately thirty seconds before Marcus pulled up and parked nearby, the way he had done each day. Excitement tightened in my chest at the sight of his blue Rav-4.

"Calm down," I muttered to myself.

He opened the driver's side door, and I expected to see his usual jacket and dress shirt. Instead, my mouth fell open as I watched him go to the back door. Moments later, an energized Noah jumped onto the sidewalk and raced toward me in his red tunic, yellow cape, and yellow utility belt, his eyes bright with joy behind the mask.

"Look, Miss Julia!"

Coming behind him with a slow but confident walk was Marcus Hayes—in a full Batman costume.

I pressed my fist to my mouth, trying hard not to laugh. He had the body to carry it off—broad shoulders, long legs, and muscular thighs. But the black cape, the purple bodysuit, the mask, and the bat symbol on his chest were *a lot* for a Friday afternoon ice cream run. He looked ridiculous yet completely adorable.

I rested my hands on my hips. "Well... Gotham's finest has made an appearance."

Noah looked at his godfather and then looked at me. "Uncle Marcus is Batman. We're a team!" he exclaimed.

"I see. This is quite an interesting look for you," I told Marcus.

He shrugged, the left corner of his mouth quirking upwards in a slightly embarrassed smile. "Robin said he needed my help, so I couldn't leave him out here fighting crime all by himself. I had to have my man's back."

Now I understood. Noah had asked him to wear the costume, and he had obliged. The fact that he'd done so at the boy's request was very endearing.

"Very noble of you, Batman."

"All in a day's work," he said, adjusting his cape with exaggerated flair.

I burst out laughing then. "Tell me you wore this all day."

"All damn day. From the time I dropped him off until now."

"All damn day!" Noah exclaimed.

"No, you don't say damn. That's a grown-up word, okay?" Marcus said.

"Okay," Noah said, sounding defeated, as if not being able to say a curse word was the worst thing ever.

"Ready for some ice cream?" Marcus asked.

"I sure am." I led the way across the street to the park, and we made our regular trek to the ice cream truck. Each day this week, Noah had tried a different flavor. So far his favorite was Rocky Road.

When we arrived at the truck, the vendor smiled at us. I wasn't surprised she was happy considering all the money Marcus had spent on ice cream and coffee this week.

"Hey, it's my favorite superhero, and you brought Batman today," she said.

"We're a team!" Noah announced again.

The vendor grinned. "What will it be today, Robin?" she asked.

"Um, I don't know. Can I have two scoops this time?" Eyes hopeful, Noah lifted his gaze to Marcus.

"You think you can eat two?"

"I know I can," the little boy said with confidence.

"All right, let's see what you got. You can have two scoops."

Noah put in his request for strawberry and cotton candy so quickly, it was clear he had been plotting to do this.

Marcus had his usual cup of coffee, but I skipped the ice cream. I realized last night I was setting myself up by eating ice cream every day, as if I were a seven-year-old boy instead of a thirty-three-year-old woman whose metabolism was not what it used to be.

We headed back across the park like we usually did, with Noah leading the way, and Marcus and I strolling behind him. Since Marcus and I were spending so much time together, I had done a Google search on him and learned he was one of the top-selling real estate agents in Houston. He had a listing coordinator and two buyer assistants, which enabled him to devote time to Noah's care early on.

While his godson sat down on a bench to finish his ice cream, Marcus and I remained standing in the grass nearby.

"How's he doing?" I asked.

"Incredibly well, except for wearing the costume. He still refuses to wear regular clothes."

"It was really sweet of you to put on the Batman costume for him."

Marcus took a sip of his coffee. "When he asked me, I couldn't say no. It's something his dad would've done. Brandon wore the costume when he took Noah trick-or-treating last year, and I guess he's been holding onto that memory."

"That could explain why he's been so attached to the Robin costume in the first place. It's a core memory."

"Exactly."

"Have his eating habits improved?"

"They have. He's finishing meals now. His appetite is back,

and of course, you've been good for him." He shot a look at me from the corner of his eye.

"Me?" He had genuinely surprised me with the compliment.

"Don't act like you don't know you're the reason we're here. I bought ice cream for him at the store, and he wouldn't eat it, but for some reason, he loves the ice cream from this truck."

"That has nothing to do with me. They make a good product. But back to your comment about me, all I do is eat ice cream with you."

"Nah, you do more than that." His voice became serious. "You consistently talk to him in an engaging way, and it's worked to pull him out of his depression. The first time he smiled was because of an interaction with you. His therapist is impressed by his progress, by the way. At his appointment on Thursday, she asked me what I was doing. When I told her I'd been taking him for ice cream, she laughed at first but sobered when she realized I was serious. 'Keep doing what you're doing,' she told me."

Warmth filled my chest. "He's a great kid, and if I helped in some small way, I'm happy."

We were silent for a moment as he drank more coffee. "His aunt called again."

Because of our daily meetups, we had developed a deeper bond, prompting him to confide in me on Wednesday about the problem he was experiencing with Noah's paternal aunt. She wanted the boy to move to Tennessee right away, but Marcus believed it was better for him to finish the school year in Houston.

Which made sense. No point in uprooting him unnecessarily and causing more disruption in his life. Besides, schools closed in about a month, so her continued insistence on having Noah move to Tennessee immediately seemed odd.

"What did she want?" I asked.

"Same shit, different day," Marcus grumbled. "I told her once and for all to accept that he's not coming to Tennessee before the end of the school year, and I think she finally got it. Then she started talking about after school closed, which I'm more open to."

"So you're going to let him go?"

"Probably," he replied, kicking a pebble onto the pavement. He didn't sound certain to me.

"I figured you might miss your little sidekick," I said carefully.

"Yeah, I'm going to miss the little guy," Marcus said, his voice sounding rougher than before. His gaze fell to Noah, who was almost finished with his ice cream.

"There's no rule that says you have to turn him over to family. Brandon and Stacey chose you to be his guardian."

"Legally, yeah, but I feel selfish for keeping him here, especially when he has family in another state. I mean, bottom line, she's right, isn't she? He's doing better now, but how much more would he thrive if he were in a stable home with other kids?"

"You underestimate what you mean to him," I said in a quiet voice.

"What do you mean?"

"Marcus, I see the way he looks at you, the way he sometimes reaches for your hand. He feels safe with you. Frankly, there's a reason your friend and his wife designated you as the guardian of their child. You should think about *that*. In my line of work, I can tell you, parents do not make such an important decision lightly."

He remained silent and took another sip of coffee before he spoke again. "I've thought about why they chose me, and I don't fully understand it, because I don't think my actions while they were alive suggested I was the best person to take care of a kid. But I have been thinking about Zenobia, his aunt. Something about her constant demand to take in Noah doesn't sit right with me. She seems almost... *desperate* to have him."

"I think we're both having the same thought."

"The insurance money," we said at the same time.

Chapter 8

Julia

"During our first conversation, she casually said, 'I'm sure Brandon made sure Noah would be well provided for.' At the time, I thought she was just making conversation, but I know better now. She's been way too persistent." Marcus sighed.

"Which is probably why they chose you to be his guardian," I pointed out. "You don't care about the money. You care about the boy."

I was too entangled in their personal affairs and had probably said too much, but I wanted to reassure Marcus that if he decided to keep Noah, he wasn't making a mistake. We should be making the best choices for his godson, and as Noah's advocate, I believed Marcus was the right choice.

Noah wandered over, his lips pushed into a pout and his brow wrinkled. "I don't feel so good."

Marcus dropped to his haunches. "What's wrong?"

"My tummy hurts," Noah said, and then he proceeded to rub his stomach.

"Too much ice cream," Marcus said in a solemn tone.

"No," Noah wailed, probably because he saw his chance of having ice cream every day slipping away.

"I think you've had enough ice cream to last you until at least the next week." Marcus stood. "We'd better go."

He said the words reluctantly, suggesting he didn't really want to leave. I didn't want him to leave, either, but I needed to get back to work and finish up some of my reports. Taking time away from my desk every day meant I had to make up the work on the backend by staying later.

Not that I minded. I enjoyed spending time with him and Noah, whom I was beginning to think of less as his godson and more like his son as I observed their interactions. That was another reason why I thought it might be a good idea for him to keep Noah here. Their relationship was growing stronger.

Noah grasped Marcus's hand and rested his head against his hip.

"I know that look. He's done for today," I remarked.

"Yeah, no doubt. Come on, Robin."

Marcus lifted Noah into his arms with ease, and the little boy flung his arms around his neck and rested his head on his shoulder. The move made my ovaries vibrate. Me, a woman who had insisted she never wanted to be a mother.

We walked to the park entrance and waited for a lull in the traffic.

"You have big plans for the weekend?" Marcus asked.

"Does doing laundry count as big plans?" I replied.

He laughed, and though the mask obscured most of his face, there was no missing those full, juicy lips of his. They were visible and entirely too appealing. And the sound of his husky laughter did things to me, making my pulse quicken despite myself.

"I figured you'd have a hot date." His eyes focused on me.

"Nothing so exciting," I told him, a little embarrassed. Now

I wished I did have plans so I wouldn't come across as lame with nothing to do all weekend.

After waiting for traffic to pass, we walked across the street and stopped in front of my building. As we faced each other, the moment felt significant. Maybe because I knew I wouldn't see them again for a while. He couldn't feed Noah ice cream every day forever, and today was Friday, which meant I wouldn't be here even if they did come tomorrow.

"It was good to see you both again, and I'm very impressed with his progress." I patted Noah's back. "I hope you feel better," I said gently.

He didn't say a word, but acknowledged me with a whimper.

"I guess I'll be stopping at the pharmacy for some kiddie Pepto-Bismol," Marcus said.

Noah lifted his head. "Miss Julia, we're going to the zoo tomorrow. Do you want to come with us?"

I blinked, surprised by the question. "The zoo?" I repeated, my gaze landing on Marcus's face.

"Don't listen to him. I'm sure you have—"

"We get to feed the goats and everything. You should come," Noah said.

"I don't think it'll be that exciting for you. We're going to the children's petting zoo," Marcus explained.

Was he trying to convince me *not* to come?

"You should come," Noah insisted. "Do you have to work?"

The expectation on his face tugged at my emotions. This sweet little boy was asking me to be part of his day. Practically speaking, I felt as if this was crossing a line. Afternoon visits were one thing, but I didn't spend time with clients on the weekend. Doing so could complicate our relationship.

"You could come... if you wanted to," Marcus said.

"Well... I don't have to work tomorrow." I looked at him, trying to gauge his true feelings.

"Then you should come with us," he said firmly.

The invitation from him sealed my decision. "I haven't been to the petting zoo before, but it sounds like a good time. Thanks for the invitation, Noah. I would love to join you." I smiled at both him and Marcus.

"Yay!" Noah said softly, raising his fisted left hand.

"What time?" I asked Marcus.

"I need to go into the office for the first part of the morning to handle some paperwork, so I was thinking about ten-thirty-ish, if that works for you? We could meet at the zoo and hang out for a couple of hours."

"Sounds good," I said, making sure I spoke in an even tone though I was jumping up and down on the inside. Not good.

I was way too excited about spending more time with Marcus and this little guy. But especially Marcus.

"Uncle Marcus said I'll get to feed the goats. Did you know that goats can climb really good? I get to see the goats and the sheep and the chickens, but I really really want to see the goats." Noah then dumped all the information he knew about goats into the conversation, though much of what he said sounded like a combination of television and imagination.

Sorry, Marcus mouthed.

I didn't mind. The kid's enthusiasm was infectious.

Finally, Marcus interrupted him. "Robin and I have to go now," he said, covering the boy's mouth mid-sentence as he was in the middle of explaining the different species of goats. "We'll see you tomorrow at the entrance to the zoo?"

"Works for me," I agreed.

I watched them walk down the sidewalk, with Noah waving over Marcus's shoulder. "Bye, Miss Julia! See you tomorrow!"

"See you tomorrow," I called back.

I watched Batman carry Robin to the vehicle and put him in the backseat. I was so focused on them, I didn't realize I was staring until Marcus had shut the door and paused to look at me. I shook out of my trance and waved.

He lifted one hand and then climbed behind the wheel.

I didn't wait until he drove off. I had been standing there long enough, so I entered my building and climbed the stairs up to the second floor. I walked briskly to my desk, ignoring Gina, who thankfully was on the phone.

I had plans this weekend. A day at the petting zoo, with Marcus and Noah.

I groaned quietly. What was I doing? I should not be getting involved with a handsome real estate agent and his adorable pseudo-son, but here we were. That's exactly what I was doing.

I sat at my desk and completed my reports, including a short summary of the progress I was seeing in Noah. As I wrote my notes, a smile crept onto my face.

He really had gone through significant change since the first time we met. This was the part of my job that I loved. The reason I got up in the morning and fought so hard for these kids.

The transformation made it all worthwhile, even the uncomfortable parts I didn't like to deal with that broke my heart, such as the abuse. Seeing them grow and become happier human beings was an immense reward. Seeing their parents or guardians also transform from being apprehensive to relaxed parents was something I appreciated. I could see Marcus becoming more comfortable as he parented Noah, and it was a beautiful thing.

Because of that, I suspected Marcus was going to have a

hard time letting him go when the school year ended. I was starting to think he wasn't going to let him go at all.

Chapter 9

Julia

I lost track of how many times I changed clothes for the trip to the petting zoo. I finally settled on a white T-shirt, jeans, and sneakers.

Normally, I wore my hair in a bun during the work week, but I allowed myself more flexibility on the weekend. I had pulled my hair into an Afro puff at the back and added lip gloss to my lips and a little mascara to my eyes to round out my look. Overall, my appearance was casual and practical, hopefully signaling that I wasn't trying too hard.

Leanne appeared in the doorway. "I see you finally decided on an outfit."

"I didn't take that long," I said, turning to check my back in the mirror. Booty looked good.

"This is me you're talking to. It's obvious you're trying to impress the hot daddy you've been eating ice cream with all week."

"First of all, I never said he was hot."

"You didn't have to. Every time you talk about them—especially him—you get this starry-eyed look on your face. Anyway, I came by to say have fun on your date."

"It's not a date! We're going to the petting zoo, and there will be a child present."

"Oh, excuse me. Have fun on your little outing to the petting zoo with a child present." She waggled her eyebrows suggestively before disappearing down the hallway.

I shook my head, laughing to myself. She was right about me taking extra time to get ready, but I refused to give her the satisfaction of knowing she was correct.

Grabbing my crossbody bag, I exited the bedroom. On the way out, I said goodbye to Leanne and the kids and hopped in my car for the drive to the petting zoo. When I arrived at the entrance, Marcus and Noah hadn't arrived yet.

Standing alone, I had time to question my decision as I watched families and single moms stroll in with their little ones. What in the world was I doing here? I should be home doing laundry like I had planned. Instead, I was waiting with bated breath for Marcus and little Noah to arrive.

"Miss Julia!"

I turned to see Noah's excited face as he ran toward me, Marcus following at a slower pace behind him. As usual, Noah was wearing his Robin costume, but Marcus wasn't Batman today. He wore dark jeans, a gray T-shirt that fit way too well, and sunglasses that hid his eyes. Dang, he looked good.

"Hey there!" I crouched down, catching Noah as he barreled into me and wrapped his arms around my neck. His enthusiastic hug made me a little emotional. He was so happy to see me, and there was something about his childlike, open, unadulterated joy that hit me in the feels. "Are you ready to see some goats?"

His smile was all teeth. "So ready! I want to see their eyes. Did you know their pupils are shaped like rectangles?"

Standing, I rested my hands on my hips. "No, but that's pretty cool."

"It helps them see all the way around so they don't have to turn their heads, and it protects them from predators."

"He watched videos on YouTube about goats all night last night," Marcus said dryly, sounding as if he had had it up to his eyeballs with the goat commentary, but his smile was warm and easy. "I know way too much about goats—more than I ever thought I would or believed was even possible."

I laughed a little.

"Goats are interesting, Uncle Marcus," Noah said, completely serious.

"I agree with him," I said.

Marcus removed the sunglasses and hooked them at the front of his shirt. "I see what's going on. Two against one, huh?"

Noah giggled. "Me and Miss Julia against you."

"Not cool." Marcus poked him twice in the side, and the little boy giggled and edged away. Then, Marcus's eyes quickly swept over me—long enough for me to notice, but short enough that it didn't seem disrespectful. "He hasn't stopped talking about this visit since you agreed to come."

"I'm happy to be here," I replied sincerely. In fact, the anxiety I had experienced while getting dressed earlier had pretty much evaporated.

"All right, let's go see these goats and chickens and whatever else they've got," Marcus said.

"Yay!" Noah threw up his hands in an exuberant cheer.

"I see he's doing much better today. No more tummy ache," I commented in a low voice.

"I convinced him that he's had enough ice cream, so I think we're going to avoid that for a little while."

"Good call," I said, though I was disappointed since it meant I wouldn't see them every day like I had been.

Marcus paid our admission, and we walked into the zoo, which was already busy with families and filled with the sounds of children squealing and laughing. Noah grabbed my hand on one side and Marcus's on the other and began swinging our joined hands.

"We're going to see the goats first, right?" Noah asked.

"Definitely goats first," Marcus confirmed, smiling at me above the boy's head.

To an outsider, we probably looked like a family—two parents smiling above the head of their kid, who happened to be dressed like a superhero.

I couldn't believe how large the petting zoo area was. The map the cashier had handed Marcus showed a huge property. In addition to the petting zoo, there was a duck pond, pony rides, and a swimming pool.

"We have to get the food," Noah said, pointing at the dispensers.

When Marcus pulled out his wallet, I waved him off. "I got it."

It was the least I could do, considering how much ice cream he had fed me during the week, and he had covered my entrance into the zoo. I fed quarters into the machine, and food pellets rattled into our plastic bucket.

We then approached a fenced enclosure with goats crowded toward the visitors feeding them. Frankly, they were rather aggressive.

"Damn," Marcus said in a low voice.

"Be careful," I warned Noah.

But he had the fearlessness of youth on his side, and he moved close, pointing at a large brown and white goat. "He's big."

A zoo volunteer was standing nearby, her hair pulled into a ponytail and long bangs covering her forehead. "That's

Munchie. He's a big guy, but he's very gentle and loves attention."

Noah poured several pellets into his palm and reached slowly toward Munchie, who ate the pellets right from his hand.

Noah looked up at us, his eyes filled with wonder. "Look! He's eating them!"

As if we couldn't see.

He giggled. This was how a seven-year-old should sound and look.

"His lips are soft," he said, pulling out more food.

"You're doing a good job of feeding him," Marcus said.

We stayed in that spot for quite a while. It was funny to see the other children staring at Noah in his costume. Some of the parents played along, pointing and making comments like, "Hey, there's Robin." Noah really enjoyed those moments and every now and again posed with his chest puffed out, arms akimbo.

After what seemed like an eternity, where Noah fed every single goat in the enclosure—including their kids—we headed to where the rabbits were located. Noah led the way with Marcus and me trailing behind him.

"He's completely different," I said in a soft voice, watching as he waved at some kids who were pointing at him.

"I know. I'm worried he'll shut down again, but he's been like this since... Wednesday, I think?"

That's when I had noticed his most marked difference, as well.

"Have you heard from his Aunt Zenobia again?"

He shook his head. "I'm hoping she's given up and will leave well enough alone."

We stopped as Noah entered the rabbit enclosure and

stood outside with parents watching their kids on the other side of the wire fence.

"For sure she can't say that he's not happy with you and well taken care of. Did you know her before your friend passed?"

"No. Brandon and I met freshman year of college, and he talked about his family, but I had only met his parents once—at graduation. Still, he and I were really close."

"I understand. I have the same relationship with my roommate. We met in middle school and we've been close ever since. She's like a sister."

"You get it. I have two sisters, so he was like a brother to me." His voice became rough. "When he asked me to be Noah's guardian, I said yes, but I never thought I'd actually have to do it. I never thought my friend would be dead at thirty-three." Beneath his beard, his jaw tightened.

"I know that must be hard."

I placed a hand on his arm and realized with a shock it was only the second time we had actually touched. His skin was warm and sprinkled with fine hairs.

His gaze found mine, and once again I experienced an odd sense of connection, as if we were the only two people present, though there were dozens of folks milling around us. There was something intensely intimate about this connection I felt we had. It wasn't imaginary. It was real and alive between us. A little scary too. I don't think I've ever experienced this type of feeling with another man.

Snatching away my hand, I broke the invisible, fragile thread connecting us. I took a breath because I needed it, and I noticed that Marcus inhaled deeply, too, as if he needed it.

"I'm glad you came today," he said, his voice sounding deeper than normal.

"I didn't have any big plans, as you know. I was literally only going to do laundry. So I didn't mind at all, even if I do smell like goat now."

He didn't speak for a while, his eyes trained on Noah, who was petting a gray rabbit. "Why did you come?"

A loaded question. "I'm concerned about Noah, and I wanted to spend more time with him and see—"

"Is Noah the only reason you're here?"

I let the question hang between us before having the courage to respond. "What are you getting at?"

"I was hoping you'd mention me."

Very direct. "Why?"

"Because I've been thinking about you a lot. More than I should."

I let out a little laugh. "You don't beat around the bush, do you?"

"I was playing it cool at first because I was concerned about Noah, but now that he's doing better, I figured I'd shoot my shot. Especially since you came today and didn't have to. So I'm asking again, why did you come?"

My heart raced as I considered lying and using Noah as an excuse again. "I like spending time with Noah," I said honestly. "And you."

A satisfied smile slipped across his lips. "If I were to ask you out..."

"If you ask me out, I'll tell you I have to think about it. At the end of the day, Noah is a client, and like you, he's my priority."

"Understood, but I do want you to think about it."

"Think about what?"

"Going out with me, so when I do ask, you give the right answer."

I raised an eyebrow at him. "And what would be the right answer?" I asked, though I already knew what he would say.

He grinned, smooth and heart-thumpingly sexy. "Yes."

Chapter 10

Marcus

Every detail about Julia's appearance had kept my attention today. The white T-shirt and jeans were simple and fit her perfectly. Her thick hair, pulled away from her face as usual, was styled in an Afro puff at the back, showing off its length and thickness.

I kept catching myself staring at her lips when she smiled or watching her eyes when she laughed at Noah's antics. Every time she crouched down to let him show her something, I focused on the curve of her neck and the way she tilted her head as she listened to him chatter on in detail about one topic or another related to the animals.

His love for animals made me think he was destined to become a veterinarian. But isn't that what every parent did when their kid showed interest in a topic? They—

My thoughts screeched to a halt.

Noah wasn't my kid, and in a few weeks, he would be traveling to Tennessee to live with family. I ignored the sadness that engulfed me whenever I considered his departure and returned my attention to the gorgeous woman in my company.

For weeks I had been in survival mode, trying to keep myself and Noah afloat. Today, watching how he interacted with Julia in a new environment and seeing how comfortable we all were together shifted my thought processes.

Noah was doing better, which freed my mind to contemplate other matters—specifically, Julia and the attraction simmering between us.

"Should we go see the sheep?" she asked, consulting the map.

"Sheep! Yes!" Noah pumped his fist in the air.

"Sounds like a plan," I replied, as if we had a choice when he reacted so enthusiastically to the suggestion.

The sheep were significantly less aggressive about the food, which seemed to disappoint Noah. He fed a few of them and then said, "They're not as much fun."

"They're definitely more polite," Julia remarked.

We moved through the rest of the petting zoo, spending time with the chickens before heading to the pond to feed the ducks. Then we came upon the area where they gave pony rides. Behind the enclosure, two kids were already on the horses. They wore helmets, and employees walked beside them.

Noah turned hopeful eyes in my direction. "Can I ride a pony?"

"Sure." I was starting to realize it was very hard to say no to this kid.

After I paid for his ride, one of the employees helped Noah onto a gentle brown pony named Chocolate. With his Robin cape draped over the animal's back, he looked absolutely thrilled, flashing a grin in my direction.

Julia and I remained outside the fence and watched him go around the little track. Every time he passed us, he waved, and we waved back.

"He's having the time of his life," she said with amusement. "I like seeing him enjoy normal kid stuff again."

"He can because of you."

I glanced at her. "You're a part of this too."

Instead of responding, she smiled softly and returned her attention to Noah, who was making another loop around the enclosure. After the ride, we wandered over to the playground area, and Noah immediately wanted to get on a swing. We had to wait for one of the kids to leave, and when they did, he rushed over.

I moved behind him and gently pushed, watching as he kicked his legs, trying to go higher. Julia remained off to the side, watching us.

"Higher!" Noah demanded.

He was freaking fearless.

"I think this is high enough," I said. When did I turn into my dad? No, my mom. My dad would've pushed me higher.

"Miss Julia, watch this!"

Before I could stop the little nut, he jumped off the swing, which, fortunately, was not too high, and landed on his feet with his arms spread wide. "Ta-da!"

"Great job, Robin," Julia said, clapping.

"Don't do that again," I said, knowing I was being a killjoy. But if I was going to send him to Tennessee at some point, I needed him to be in one piece. "Let's go, Robin. Other kids want to use the swing."

He raced past me toward Julia. "Did you see me?"

"I saw you."

I shook my head. "Stop encouraging him."

"I'm not!" she said.

"I'm not!" I repeated, mimicking the softness of her voice.

She slammed her hands on her hips. "Are you making fun of me?"

"No." She was so cute, trying to act like she was mad.

While we were busy talking, Noah had climbed onto a colorful structure on the playground. I didn't know where he was getting the energy. I glanced at Julia, who was watching him. I didn't want the day to end. I didn't want to go back to the condo where it was just me and Noah. I wanted more time with her and more time to explore whatever was happening between us.

Finally, Noah finished his climbing and came running over. "I'm hungry," he announced.

I made a big show of checking the watch on my wrist. "It's after lunchtime, and I'm getting hungry too. Are you hungry?" I asked Julia. "We could grab a bite to eat at the café near the entrance. My treat."

I held my breath. I wanted her to say yes to spending a little more time with us.

"I could eat," she said.

"Can we get pizza?" Noah asked.

"Let's see what they have first," I said, resting my hand on his head as he fell into step beside me. "We've had pizza twice this week. They probably have hotdogs and other options."

"The two of you like pizza, I take it?" Julia asked.

"It's an easy meal," I explained.

"Uncle Marcus doesn't know how to cook," Noah said, putting me on blast.

"Damn, bro."

Julia hid her laughter behind her hand.

"But you don't. Can you cook, Miss Julia?"

"Yes, I can cook since I'm not like your Uncle Marcus. I can't eat anything I want and not gain weight," she said.

"I was blessed with a high metabolism." I patted my stomach.

Her eyes drifted to the same spot, lingered, and then skittered away.

Yeah, she wanted me.

Since we arrived at the café after the lunchtime rush, we were able to snag a table near a window. Noah decided on a hotdog and fries, and he attacked the meal as if I hadn't been feeding him. Julia and I both had burgers and fries.

"So," I said, keeping my tone casual. "How come you don't have a man?"

I should probably mind my own business, but sitting across from her, with the afternoon light hitting her face and making her already burnished skin appear brighter, I couldn't help myself.

She raised an eyebrow. "Why are you all up in my business?"

I laughed and shrugged. "I'm curious. You're a smart, beautiful woman who is great with kids. I can't believe someone hasn't swept you up already."

She shot a quick glance at Noah, who was preoccupied with his food and humming to himself. "I don't want any."

Kids? Shocked, I mouthed the word.

She confirmed with a nod. Honestly, I couldn't believe it. She was so good with them. There was also another sensation coursing through me. Disappointment. Which was odd, because before Noah entered my life, I never considered being a father myself.

"Why not?"

"Too much responsibility. Don't get me wrong, I love them, but... I see so much dysfunction all day in my work, I guess I don't want to risk dealing with the same problems in my personal life."

I didn't understand. Few people were better equipped to

handle the challenges of being a parent than the woman sitting directly across from me.

"Is that why you're single? You haven't found someone who shares your view about children?" I asked.

Julia dipped a fry in ketchup and ate it. "It is hard to find someone like that, but I thought I had found him. We were serious for a few years and split a couple of years ago. He accepted a job offer in Portland and wanted me to move with him."

"But you didn't want to go?"

"I love Houston. My job is here, my friends are here, my whole life is here. I wasn't ready to give all that up for a relationship where there was no certainty. He didn't ask me to marry him. He asked me to uproot my life and come live with him, and there was uncertainty in that—at least for me." She took a sip of Coke before continuing. "We tried long distance for a while, but it didn't work out. Since then, I've learned to be on my own."

"Lucky me." The words slipped out. They should've stayed in my head, but I wasn't sorry I had expressed how I felt.

When her eyes met mine, the current hummed between us again. Palpable. Undeniable.

"Uncle Marcus, can I have dessert?" Noah asked.

His question snapped the connection.

"Yes. What do you want?" I wiped ketchup from his cheek with a napkin.

"Ice cream?" he asked, his voice rising with hope.

I laughed. "Nice try. Remember our deal? You've had enough ice cream for the week."

His face fell. "Okay," he muttered, pouting.

"How about a cookie? They have chocolate chip."

He nodded vigorously, perking up. "I like chocolate chip."

As soon as he said it, I remembered chocolate chip was his

favorite. Stacey always had chocolate chip cookies in the pantry. I made a mental note to buy some to keep at the condo as a treat for him.

We finished eating, and I bought the cookie on the way out.

"We're going to walk Miss Julia to her car," I told Noah.

"Why?" he asked, biting into the cookie.

"Because we have to make sure she gets to her car safely, which is the gentlemanly thing to do. We always want to be gentlemen when there's a lady present. Got it?"

He nodded, immediately serious. "Got it."

We made our way toward the parking lot, with me walking between Noah and Julia. In between cookie bites, he chattered about all the goats he had met and how he was going to draw pictures of them when we got home. I had snapped a few photos of him feeding the animals, which I would show him later.

He slipped his hand in mine, small and warm and trusting. Julia's hand swung near mine on the other side. I longed to take it, but that would be too much. We hadn't even gone on a proper date yet.

We arrived at her gray Nissan Sentra far too soon, and she unlocked the door but didn't get in immediately. She gave Noah a hug, then straightened and looked at me. Our eyes held for a beat, a whole conversation taking place without words being exchanged.

"I enjoyed my time today," she said in a soft voice.

The words *I haven't stopped thinking about you once this week, not even when we were apart* were on the tip of my tongue, but I couldn't say them. Not with Noah standing right beside us, looking at us with curious eyes.

"I did too."

I pulled her into my arms and experienced one of the best hugs I've ever had. She was soft and warm, and even after half a day outside, smelled like heaven. I rubbed my hands up and down her back twice before letting her go.

"Drive safely."

"I will." Her voice shook a little, and I understood why. We were both falling. Whatever emotion she felt was also charging through me, leaving me a bit unsteady on my feet.

She climbed into the car, and as she started the engine, I placed a hand on Noah's shoulder and guided him to step back. We watched her back out of the parking space and drive toward the exit.

When she finally disappeared from view, Noah slipped his hand into mine.

"I already miss her," he said quietly.

With my chest tight, I squeezed his hand. "Yeah. Me too."

Chapter 11

Marcus

Monday morning, I rolled out of bed at six-thirty like I had been doing for the past few weeks and stumbled into the kitchen to start the coffee maker before waking up Noah. Once I had finished my own morning routine, I went into his room.

"Let's go, big man. Time to get ready for school," I said, shaking him gently.

He moaned, rubbing his eyes as he yawned.

After ensuring he had brushed his teeth properly, I headed back to the kitchen and placed a couple of strawberry Pop-Tarts in the toaster, our standard breakfast. I wasn't going to win father of the year, but at least he was getting food in his belly.

Nonetheless, I intended to learn how to cook. His comment at the petting zoo had been jarring. He was a growing kid and needed vegetables and home-cooked meals. Last night, I bookmarked a couple of YouTube videos that showed how to make simple dishes like spaghetti and meat sauce, and my sister promised to send over a couple of easy recipes later this week.

While the coffee brewed, I checked my morning schedule. I had a client meeting at eleven and needed to complete some paperwork. My listing coordinator, Lupe, was doing a great job handling work when I couldn't be in the office, but I couldn't have her covering for me indefinitely. It wouldn't be fair.

"Uncle Marcus?"

Noah was standing in the kitchen doorway, already dressed. But instead of the Robin costume I had washed and placed in his dresser, he was wearing khaki pants and a white shirt, which was crooked because he had missed one of the buttonholes.

"Hey, you're already dressed. Good job." I walked over to him and dropped onto my haunches. I started fixing the buttons. "Where's your costume?"

"I don't want to wear it today."

I paused in the middle of working on the second button to look into his eyes. He had been Robin for weeks.

"Why not?"

"I want to wear a tie, like you."

Emotion clogged my throat as I realized he was dressed somewhat like me. Today I was wearing khaki pants, a dress shirt, a tie, and a jacket.

"You want to wear a tie?"

"Yes. Can I?"

I didn't have a kid's tie and hadn't even thought about getting one, but Noah was looking at me with his big brown eyes full of hope and what looked suspiciously like admiration. If I could, I would've bought out every tie in the Houston department stores.

I continued working on the buttons. "I don't have a tie that can fit you right now, buddy. But you know what we can do? After I pick you up from school today, we'll go shopping and buy a couple. How does that sound?"

His face lit up. "Really?"

"Really. That way you'll have options, depending on what you wear." I finished fixing his shirt and tucked it into his pants. Then I stood and stepped back, eyeing him critically. "You know what though? You look pretty darn sharp, even without the tie."

He straightened his spine and smoothed his shirt. "Thanks. I want to look like you."

Geez, this kid. "I appreciate the compliment."

"And you take care of me really good." His voice softened. "Daddy would be happy."

I lowered to his level again and pulled him into a hug, holding him tight while blinking back the burning in my eyes. This place was so freaking dusty. "I'm doing my best, and I think your dad would be proud of you too. You're doing a really good job. You're so brave and strong."

"Can I still wear the Robin costume sometimes if I want to?"

"You sure can. Whenever you want." We sealed the deal with a fist bump.

He sat down and had Pop-Tarts and orange juice, his legs swinging under the table. Later, after I dropped him off at school, I went by one of the houses we had sold to pick up my signs from the yard before the new family moved in. On the way to the office, I decided to give Julia a ring and ask her about going out with me. I had intended to wait until later in the week, but why wait? I knew she was feeling me just as much as I was feeling her.

Before I could call, my phone rang, and it was my frat brother, Jashaun. There were three of us who had pledged on the same line and were still tight—me, Jashaun, and Elijah. Jashaun was the most social of us and the one most in tune to the frat's activities post-graduation. He had recently found out he was the father to a little girl. Elijah also had a little girl, who he parented alone after his wife left.

"Yo, what's up?" I signaled to pass into the next lane.

"Nothing, man. I know you've been busy taking care of Noah. How's he doing?"

I gave him an update on my godson's progress and the trip to the zoo over the weekend.

"He's really improving," he remarked.

"It's incredible. His therapist says he's not completely out of the woods yet, but she is impressed by the change in his behavior and wants to continue seeing him for a while longer."

"Isn't he supposed to move to Tennessee next month?"

"Yeah, I've been thinking about that. I'm going to tell Zenobia that I want to wait so he can continue with therapy for a couple more months at least. I talked to the therapist about it, and she agrees that waiting is best."

"His aunt isn't going to like that."

"Doesn't matter what she likes. All that matters is what's best for Noah, and I'm always going to do what's best for him."

"That's what's up. Good luck dealing with her though. You already have your hands full taking care of him, and having her give you a hard time doesn't help."

"I'm handling the situation for now."

"Hey, remember the organization I told you about, the Single Dad Society?"

He had mentioned them before I started caring for Noah, so it had slipped my mind. "Yeah, I had forgotten about them."

Jashaun worked for the city and had reviewed their proposal when they put in a bid for a permanent spot at a community center in town. They received approval, and he had joined the organization and encouraged Elijah to join. Both of them had praised the society for the support they provided to single fathers around the country.

"They're the other reason I'm calling. They have events every month, and when the weather's nice, they plan outdoor activities. There's one in a few weeks—Grill and Play Day at Levy Park. You should come. I'll have my daughter, and Elijah's bringing his daughter. The group will have all kinds of activities planned for the kids, so Noah should enjoy himself, and you'll have a chance to meet some of the other men and learn more about the organization."

That sounded good to me, and I knew how much support the group provided. Attorney members often donated hours to provide legal counsel to fathers who wanted more time with their kids.

"I'll be there. Text me the info."

"Done."

By the time we hung up, I was pulling into the Houston Realty parking lot. Before going inside, I dialed Julia's number. A bout of nerves hit me, but I pressed send and waited to hear her sweet voice.

"Good morning, Marcus."

A grin spread across my face. I couldn't believe how hard I was cheesing. "Good morning. Do you have any idea why I'm calling?"

"No, not really," she said in a guarded voice.

"I'm ready for you to give me an answer on whether or not you'll go out with me."

"I thought I'd have more time."

I could hear the smile in her voice and the change in how she spoke. Women always developed a sing-song voice when they were pleased but trying to hide it.

"I can't wait any longer. I need an answer." I was talking big and bold, conveying more confidence than I felt. I had asked women out hundreds of times before, but this was different. More important. As if the stakes were higher. "I was thinking dinner on Saturday at a really nice restaurant."

"Sounds fancy."

"I can't cook, but I can do fancy. So what do you think? You, me, a white tablecloth, a nice restaurant, and some good food?"

"What about Noah?"

"I'm going to check with his old babysitter, Mrs. Patterson. She always babysat Noah whenever his parents wanted a night out, and he's familiar with her. I can drop him off with her while we go out to eat and then pick him up when we're done—unless you want him to join us?"

"I think an adults-only evening sounds nice." Her voice remained warm and inviting.

"Is that a yes?"

In my opinion, it took way too long for her to answer, but in reality, only seconds passed.

"Yes, and Saturday works."

Excitement rushed through me. "I'll call you later in the week with the details."

"How dressed up should I be?"

"I'm taking you someplace where I have to wear a jacket and tie, so I'd suggest a nice dress. But sweetheart, you could wear a potato sack and you'd still look beautiful."

"You're such a smooth talker."

I chuckled softly. "I try. I gotta run, but I'll reach out in a couple of days."

After we hung up, I walked into the building, my mood much lighter than I had been in a very long time. Julia was different from other women I had been involved with in the past. I never cared to let any of them get close, but I felt as if she understood Noah *and* me. She wasn't just pretty. She made everything better with her presence.

When I walked into the office, my listing coordinator, Lupe, narrowed her eyes as she followed me into my office.

"Why are you looking at me like that?" I asked, dropping my satchel on my desk.

"You have a certain look about you, as if you asked a pretty girl out and she said yes." She handed me a manila folder. She had no idea how on target her suspicions were.

"What's this?"

"The Jacksons countered, but they're willing to increase the offer by five thousand if the sellers include the appliances."

I opened the folder and forced my attention to the words on the paper instead of thinking about Julia and our plans for Saturday. I wanted to impress her and had a few ideas of places to take her.

"Thanks. I'll let the seller know." I rounded the desk and sat in my chair.

"By the way, whatever you have going on, I'm happy for you."

I raised my eyebrows. "I figured you'd be upset you have all this extra work to do."

"To be honest, I like the extra work. It's good experience because one of these days I want to do what you do. Besides, you seem happier. I guess things are going well with the *niñito*?"

I suddenly realized that I had a whole village of people who cared about me and Noah and wanted what was best for us. Just this morning, including Lupe, I talked to three people who had shown interest in our welfare.

"Much better. He's thriving."

As she walked away, I felt as if my life was turning a corner. Business was good with Lupe and my other assistants holding down the fort. I was going to get involved with the Single Dad Society, which would expand my village and could prove helpful in the next few months as I worked with Noah. Because I wasn't going to let him go to Tennessee and have his therapy sessions disrupted. Zenobia would have to deal.

Then there was Julia, another bright spot in my life.

Saturday couldn't come fast enough.

Chapter 12

Marcus

It was late afternoon when Noah and I walked toward McDonald's. We had gone tie shopping at the mall and visited several stores before we found what he liked at Macy's. I can't believe how picky a seven-year-old was, but he had good taste. He wanted us to match, so of the three ties I purchased for him, I bought two in the same color for me. I'll never forget how he held onto the bag with both hands as we walked out of the store, as if the plastic contained an object more precious than gold.

Now it was time for dinner. We were both hungry, and McDonald's was on the way home. Noah ordered a Happy Meal with chicken nuggets, and I ordered a Big Mac combo. We sat in a booth near the window and dug into our meals.

"How was school today?"

I had waited to ask him this question so I could closely watch his expression. Though he was doing much better, the therapist had said he wasn't completely out of the woods yet, so I wanted to catch any flicker of trouble since he might not express any issues out loud.

He told me about his day, the Reading Corner, and how he had read a funny book called *The Cat in the Hat.* His conversation was normal and animated, which allayed my fears.

"Hey, buddy, I wanted to talk to you about this coming weekend. On Saturday night, I'm going out. I'm going to take you to see Mrs. Patterson. You haven't seen her in a while."

"Okay." Noah ate a few fries. "Are you going on a date?"

I wasn't sure how much to tell him. He was only seven, after all. Should I tell him I was seeing Julia? Probably not. At least not yet, until we figured out where our relationship was going. "Yes, I'm going on a date."

"How long will you be gone?"

"Not long. A couple of hours, and then I'll be back to get you."

I had called Mrs. Patterson earlier to make sure she was available. Thankfully, she was, and I'd scored a reservation at a high-end restaurant, too, so my plans were coming together for the night out with Julia.

Noah and I ate in silence for a few minutes, and then he pushed aside his box, leaving behind half his nuggets and half his fries.

"You finished already? You still have a lot more to eat."

"I'm full."

"Are you sure?" He had told me he was hungry in the car.

"I'm sure." His voice sounded smaller. Maybe he was tired. With school and then going from store to store to find the perfect ties, he'd had a long day.

"All right, big man. I'm going to the front to grab a bag so we can take this home. You might want it later."

I slid out of the booth, went to the counter, and asked for a to-go bag. The teenager behind the register scowled at me in annoyance and made me wait before handing over a paper sack. Her stank attitude couldn't affect my good mood, though.

"Thank you," I said with a smile.

I headed back to the table, but when I saw the booth was empty, I stopped short.

I scanned the restaurant. "Noah?" I called out to no one in particular.

Maybe he had gone to the bathroom. This McDonald's was one of the few that still had an indoor playground. Maybe he had gone in there to play.

First, I checked the playground but only saw a couple of kids I didn't recognize climbing through the tunnels. Unease built in my body. I walked briskly to the bathroom and pushed open the door.

"Noah? Are you in here?"

The empty bathroom echoed my voice back to me, and my stomach dropped. I was starting to freak out.

"Noah!" I yelled his name, and some of the customers stared at me.

I checked the empty booths. A woman sitting with two toddlers eyed me as if I were a lunatic.

"Have you seen a little Black boy? He's seven years old, wearing khaki pants and a white shirt?"

She shook her head. "No, I'm sorry. I haven't seen him."

I asked the couple sitting by the window, but they hadn't seen him either.

Did no one pay attention to their surroundings anymore?

Where the hell could he be?

I pushed through the front doors into the parking lot and listened to the roar of traffic going by as my heart hammered my ribs. My eyes flitted back and forth.

"Noah!" I bellowed.

A white sedan cruised by on its way to the drive-through. The parking lot itself was filled with vehicles, all places for a small boy to hide.

"*Noah*!"

Had someone snatched him while my back was turned?

My hand shook as I removed my phone from my pocket. I needed help, and the first person who came to mind was Julia. Then I saw a flash of white running along the sidewalk on the opposite side of the road, his little legs pumping as fast as they could carry him.

Noah! How did he get over there without getting run over by a car?

Terror froze me for a moment, and then I was sprinting across the parking lot. I barely registered the Toyota that honked at me as I dodged in front of it. I ran into traffic, lifting a hand toward a pickup truck barreling toward me. The driver slammed the brakes and jolted to a halt. He leaned on his horn, yelling and cursing, but I didn't hear a word.

I raced across another lane of traffic, grateful for the vehicles that slowed when they saw me. As my foot hit the sidewalk, I yelled, "Noah!"

He kept running, but his short legs were no match for my longer ones. Within seconds, I reached him and grabbed him by the shoulders.

"Hey!" I forcefully swung him around to face me. "What the hell is wrong with you? What were you thinking?" I demanded, harshly and loudly. "You don't just run off like that. Do you have any idea how scared I was? You could've been hit by a car. You could've—"

Noah was crying. Sobbing. His whole body was shaking. Tears streamed down his face.

"What's wrong? Talk to me, buddy."

"You were going to leave me *forever*!" he screamed, the words breaking apart as his breath came out in hiccupping gasps.

"What?"

He rubbed his eyes, still shaking. "Y-you s-said you were going on a date. You were—you were going to leave me with Mrs. Patterson and n-never come back. Just like M-mommy and D-daddy. They went on a date and n-never came b-back for me!"

Brandon and Stacey had left him with the babysitter. They had probably kissed him goodbye and said they'd be back after a few hours, and then they had died. They had never come back for him. I had told him I was going to do something similar.

How had I not picked up on his anxiety? I dropped to my knees in front of him and yanked him into my arms. He didn't put his arms around me, as if he was afraid to hug me back.

"You s-said—"

"I said I was going on a date for a few hours. I was going to have dinner, and I was going to come right back to get you. I promise."

"Mommy and Daddy said they were c-coming back too," he said in a small, broken voice.

Validate his pain.

I pulled back and cupped his tear-streaked face. "When I said I was going on a date, you got scared. You thought I'd leave you and you'd be all alone again."

He nodded, his lower lip trembling.

"I was only going out for a few hours. I would *never* leave you alone forever."

His lower lip trembled. "You promise?"

"I promise." I pulled him into my arms again, and this time he buried his face in my neck and fisted my shirt, sobbing as if in relief. "I don't need to go anywhere on Saturday. I'm going to stay home with you, buddy."

I don't know how long we stayed like that as he cried. People passed us on the sidewalk and cars drove by. I held him the entire time, letting him cry, tears burning hot behind my own eyes.

When his sobs finally quieted to sniffles, I stood and lifted him with me. He wrapped his legs around my waist and his arms around my neck, clinging to me, afraid to let me go.

I waited until the light changed and crossed the street with him in my arms. At the car, I gently unlatched his limbs and placed him in the backseat. Then I climbed behind the steering wheel.

Our food was sitting on the table at McDonald's, but I didn't go back for it. I just drove home. During the short ride, Noah was quiet in the backseat. I kept checking on him by looking in the rearview mirror. We were almost to my condo when his small voice broke the silence.

"Uncle Marcus?" His voice was hoarse from all the crying.

"Yeah, buddy?" I glanced at his little face in the mirror.

"I love you."

Geez, this kid.

His words hit me square in the chest, and my vision blurred. I had to blink rapidly to clear it, but a single tear escaped and slipped down my cheek. I roughly swiped it away with my knuckles.

Reaching back blindly, I found his small foot and gently squeezed it. "I love you too. So much." My voice came out thick and trembled.

When I pulled into the parking garage below my building, I sat there for a while with the engine turned off and my hands on the steering wheel. Noah had fallen asleep, his face peaceful. The long day and all that crying had drained him.

I climbed out of the car and retrieved the Macy's bag from the trunk. I stared at it for a moment, thinking about our matching ties and how excited he had been about wearing one to school.

I still didn't know if I could do this. If I was enough. But that evening, I had made Noah a promise that I wouldn't leave him, and that was the truth. This arrangement wasn't temporary. I wasn't going to leave him. I wasn't going to let him go.

He was my son, and I was his dad, and our arrangement was permanent. Almost losing him tonight made me realize how much he meant to me. I had been *terrified*, and I had never known that type of horror in my life. I never wanted to know it again. More than anything, I never wanted him to know loss again—the kind he experienced when his parents never came back for him.

So I would have to figure this out, including the situation with Zenobia.

I opened the back door and carefully unbuckled Noah. He stirred a little as I lifted him. Automatically, his little arms wrapped around my neck, and his head settled on my shoulder.

I took him up in the elevator, smiling at one of the residents who joined us when the cabin stopped on the ground floor.

Once we were home, I removed his clothes and left him in his underwear. I didn't bother putting on his pajamas and pulled the sheets over him. I sat on the edge of the bed, watching him sleep and listening to his breathing.

The weight of his disappearance had hit me hard.

I had almost lost him.

We were family now, but we were still figuring out our life together—one terrifying event at a time.

I turned off the light beside his bed and quietly left the room.

Chapter 13

Julia

I was in the middle of typing case notes when my phone rang with a call from our front desk coordinator.

"Hi, Julia. You have a visitor."

"Who is it?" I didn't have any appointments this afternoon.

"His name is Marcus Hayes, and he said it's important." She spoke in a low voice, suggesting he was probably standing near her desk.

My fingers tightened around the phone. What was Marcus doing at my office? On Tuesday morning, I received a text from him where he abruptly canceled our Saturday night date without explanation. Since then, I had been convincing myself the cancellation didn't matter. I told myself it was better this way instead of getting involved with a client's guardian and crossing a line I probably shouldn't cross.

He had a right to change his mind, but I was still hurt, and since there hadn't been any follow-up, his silence confirmed what I had been thinking. Getting involved with him was too complicated, too messy, and a bad idea in general. His line name was Romeo, for goodness' sake!

So what was he doing here?

Despite my reservations, I closed my laptop. "Tell him I'll be right out."

I took a moment to collect myself, smoothing down my blouse and taking a deep breath, reminding myself to be professional and not show emotion. Then I left my desk and walked into the reception area.

Marcus was standing with his hands shoved into his pockets, head bent as he studied the carpeted floor. When he heard me enter, he lifted his eyes, and I noted exhaustion on his face and dark circles under his eyes. When he smiled, it seemed to take a bit of effort.

I immediately felt sorry for him and was worried. Could something have happened to Noah? Since I didn't know for sure, I steeled myself for the upcoming conversation.

"Hi, Marcus."

He walked over, studying me with unnerving intensity. "Hi. I was wondering if we could go somewhere private and talk."

He shot a surreptitious glance at the receptionist, who was doing a poor job of pretending not to listen. I considered saying no and demanding he tell me what he wanted to say right then and there, but I didn't need her in my personal business.

"We can meet in the conference room."

He followed me down the hall into the small room, and I closed the door behind us. We stood facing each other with unusual awkwardness.

I crossed my arms over my chest. "What did you have to tell me?"

"I need to explain why I had to cancel our date on Saturday."

I smiled. Though I couldn't see myself, I knew my expression was tight and unnatural. "You don't need to explain. You changed your mind. No big deal. I understand." I kept my voice cool and detached.

His eyebrows drew together in consternation. "That's not what happened."

"Look, I don't have time for games. I should've known better, anyway, since you call yourself Romeo, and we shouldn't have made plans given that Noah is a client of mine. No need to apologize if that's what you were about to do. It's actually best that we don't get involved."

"Is that what you really believe?"

I shrugged. What I said wasn't what I believed, but I was trying to save face.

He took a breath. "I canceled on you for a good reason, but I couldn't go into details at the time. I had a lot going on. There was an incident with Noah."

My worst fear had been realized. The minute he mentioned the little boy's name, he had my attention. "What happened?"

"He and I went tie shopping after school the other day, and we had a really good afternoon together. We found a couple of ties that he liked, and on the way home, we stopped at McDonald's for dinner. I told him I had plans on Saturday night and that he was going to stay at Mrs. Patterson's for a few hours while I went on a date."

I watched his features shift into a pained expression.

"He didn't finish his food, and then one of the worst things that has ever happened to me took place."

He explained that Noah left the restaurant while he was at the front getting a bag for the leftover food. He told me how Noah was across the street when he finally saw him, essentially running away. When he told me what the little boy said when he finally caught up with him, I gasped, my hand going to my mouth.

"He thought I was going to drop him off and never come back like his parents did."

My heart cracked open a little. "That poor baby. Marcus, I'm so sorry."

"He wouldn't stop crying, which ripped me wide open." He ran a hand over the back of his head.

I stepped closer, my detachment crumbling at the sight of his agitation. "How is he now?"

"Better, but I'm worried about his abandonment issues, and the therapist is concerned as well. We've been seeing her the past couple of days after school. He's just been my priority, but I wanted to talk to you in person to explain what happened."

To think, I had been angry and hurt when he had been dealing with so much. "How are you?"

He smiled in a half-sexy way, not his full-on sexy grin that had made me weak-kneed in the past.

"Better than two nights ago."

We both laughed, easing the tension in the room.

His expression became earnest, and he moved a step closer. "I really want to spend time with you, Julia. I wasn't just saying that, and I wasn't playing games. I'm not going to lie and pretend I haven't done some foul shit in my past, but I care about you. *A lot.* But right now, I don't want to leave Noah. I don't think he's ready."

"I understand. He comes first and he's your priority." I could never fault a parent for prioritizing the care of their child. It was expected and exactly what I would do in his position.

"Seeing as I want to spend time with you but we can't go out on a date, I was wondering if you would consider coming to my place. Noah already called me out, so you know I can't cook. I figured we could order pizza or something and watch a movie. How does that sound?"

Studying his face, I saw hope and raw vulnerability in his

eyes. He had driven across town to explain in person and ask for another chance. How could I resist that kind of effort?

"Your idea of a relaxing evening at your place sounds perfect."

"So it's a date?" I could hear his confidence returning.

"Yes, it's a date."

"Same time, then. Noah will probably eat dinner with us, watch some of the movie, and then fall asleep like he always does. Once I put him down, we'll have time alone."

"Works for me."

As we fell silent, it dawned on me that we were standing very close. So close I could see the lighter shades of brown in his dark eyes and smell the inviting fragrance of his cologne.

He reached out and let his fingers brush mine. When I didn't pull away, he held onto my hand and pulled me toward him while at the same time stepping closer.

"As usual, talking to you makes all the bad things better," he whispered.

"I've told you before, you're doing an amazing job."

"Maybe, though I didn't feel that way when I saw him running across the street. I know this isn't the time or place, but I want to kiss you so bad, and I don't want to wait until Saturday."

I cocked my head to the side. "What makes you think you'll be able to kiss me on Saturday?"

Slowly, he smiled, his confidence fully returned. "I'm going to kiss you on Saturday, and I'm going to kiss you today," he informed me.

His confidence was like an aphrodisiac. As he bent his head toward mine, I never once considered denying him.

The connection of our lips was soft and tentative at first, as if we were both testing the waters while doing something we had no business doing at my workplace. I leaned into him, my hands lifting to his shoulders as the kiss deepened. Marcus's right hand cupped the back of my head, his fingers sinking into my bun and holding my head in place.

I made a sound that was part sigh and part moan, feeling him smile against my mouth. His left arm wound around my waist, pulling me closer. With our bodies pressed tightly together, I felt every hard inch of him—from his chest to his powerful thighs—and the hardening bulge pressed against my abdomen.

His tongue teased the seam of my lips, and I opened for him, plunging my own tongue into his mouth. I tasted coffee combined with the delicious flavor that was all Marcus.

Gripping his shirt, I anchored myself while the Earth shifted beneath my feet. Angling his head to the side, he devoured my mouth as our tongues tangled and stoked the flames of desire.

One hand lowered to grab my bottom, while the other tightened in my hair, tilting my head back to deepen the kiss. Heat scorched my blood. I knew he would be a good kisser, but this was devastatingly good. It was the kind of kiss that made you forget your own name and where you were.

I caressed his nape and slid my hand up the back of his head. As he ground his hips against mine, I groaned softly, almost angry at the unfulfilled promise in his movements. Yes, we were in my office, but I couldn't make myself care.

His lips left mine to trail a path along my jaw to the sensitive spot below my ear, and I let out an open-mouthed gasp that was louder than I intended. Digging my fingers into his shoulders, I rubbed my aching nipples against his chest and heard a rumble of male approval.

"Damn, Julia," he murmured against my neck, his voice hoarse and unrecognizable.

Hearing my name broke the spell of hazy lust I had fallen under, and I remembered with a jolt where we were.

I placed a hand on his chest and felt his heart racing beneath my palm as I gently pushed him back. "I think that's enough for today," I said with a shaky laugh.

He stepped back reluctantly, licking his thick lips, his breathing as ragged as mine, looking very much like he wanted to finish what we'd started.

I touched my fingers to my throbbing mouth, where the phantom pressure of his kiss remained.

He looked me up and down, his nostrils notably flaring. "I better go before I lift you onto that table and do things that will get you fired."

Heat flashed through me at the visual he created, and I shook my head to dispel the image of me on the table, my skirt shoved up to my thighs. Marcus between my legs, pumping his hips and giving me exactly what I craved.

"Good idea. I'll see you on Saturday."

"You best believe you'll see me on Saturday. If you don't show up, Noah and I are jumping in the car to come find you."

"I promise I'll be there," I said with a smile.

Slipping his hand into my waistband, he pulled me in for a short, hot kiss. "I should go before I change my mind and follow through on my threat," he said against my lips. Another quick kiss. "I'll talk to you later."

Then he left.

I remained behind, standing in the conference room with kiss-swollen lips and a racing heart, wondering how I was supposed to concentrate on work for the rest of the day.

Chapter 14

Julia

Yet again, getting dressed to see Marcus had me trying on different outfits. My black dress was too formal, and my wrap dress implied I was trying too hard. I settled on a burgundy wrap tank top and jeans. According to Leanne, I looked sexy.

"He's going to lose his mind," she said from the doorway of my bathroom.

No doubt I looked good because Leanne would have told me if I didn't. It was nice to have someone I could trust completely.

"Thanks." I fluffed my hair, admiring the volume of my twist-out. I added dangling earrings to my ears, and my look was complete.

I turned to face her, overcome with sadness. She and the girls were moving out tomorrow. She and her husband had both been playing a game of chicken, neither wanting to be the one to give in first, but the last time he came to pick up the girls, he dropped to his knees and begged Leanne to come home.

"How much more do you have to pack?" I asked.

"I'm at the point where I'm tossing clothes into trash bags because I. Am. Tired." She blew out a breath.

I pouted. "It's going to be awfully quiet around here after you guys leave."

"Please, we've been crowding you in your space. I'm sure you'll be happy to have your living room back and a quiet apartment when you come home after a long day at work."

"Don't be too sure. I kind of liked being handed a glass of wine when I walked in the door and having a hot meal waiting for me."

We both laughed and then slowly sobered. I'd miss them, but I was glad she and her husband had reconciled, and he promised to be more present and considerate of her feelings moving forward.

"I better go before I'm late." I sprayed perfume on my wrists and neck, the latter reminding me of how Marcus's lips had caressed my sensitive skin. My inner thighs tingled from the memory.

I grabbed my purse. "Bye," I said as I headed to the front door.

"Have fun!" Leanne said.

"Bye, Aunt Julia!" the girls hollered.

The drive to Marcus's condo didn't take long. When I arrived, he opened the door with a smile and gave me a hug. I pressed myself against him, enjoying the warmth of his embrace and his clean, masculine smell.

"Where's Noah?" I asked as I stepped inside. He had a nice open floor plan, with modern furniture and windows that provided an impressive view of the Houston skyline. The place was clean and organized, but I saw evidence of a child in the home. Noah's backpack was on a stand near the door, his drawings were mounted on the front of the refrigerator with magnets, and a pile of toys was stuffed into a corner of the living room.

"I told him you were coming, but he already fell asleep," Marcus said, pointing.

Sure enough, Noah was curled up under a blanket on the sofa.

"How's he been doing?" I whispered, placing my purse on a table beside the sofa.

"According to the therapist, he's going to be fine. She said I'm doing all the right things to reassure him."

I was really impressed by Marcus's dedication. He seemed like the typical bachelor, but rather than having his life upended by the responsibility of taking care of a child, somehow he had managed to pivot and embrace his role as a surrogate parent.

"I ordered the pizza about thirty minutes ago, so it should be here soon. I'll put him to bed, and we can have a drink while we wait. Wine good?"

"Wine or a beer or juice or whatever you have is fine by me."

"You drink beer?" he asked, sounding surprised.

"Oh yeah. I'm a Full Moon girlie. I love everything the Johnson family put out, including the specialty flavors around different holidays."

"See, I knew I liked you. That's my favorite brand too. I have a couple of bottles of their lager in the refrigerator. Help yourself while I put him to bed."

As he carefully picked up Noah, I went into the kitchen and helped myself to one of his bottled brews. Tilting back my head, I took a big sip and examined the pictures on the door of the stainless steel refrigerator.

"Those top two he made in school, and the other four he

drew here. I let him decide which ones he thinks are the best, and we put those on the refrigerator."

"He has real talent. I can actually see that's a goat, and those are sheep and ducks. When my goddaughter Paige draws a picture, I can't decipher what she drew. I always feel like I'm looking at hieroglyphics."

"Not hieroglyphics," Marcus said with a laugh.

"I'm afraid so."

We both fell silent.

"I can't believe you're actually here in my house. You look amazing. I like your hair like that."

"Thanks," I said, feeling a little bashful.

He edged closer and kissed my cheek. Then he inhaled deeply. "You smell good too," he added huskily.

Maybe it was because of the kiss at my workplace, but there seemed to be an inordinate amount of sexual tension between us. I touched his firm chest. "How much do you work out?"

"I used to be a fanatic, but I don't go to the gym as much anymore, especially since..."

"Noah entered your life?"

"Yeah. I used to go after work, but I need to figure out how to reincorporate exercise into my schedule. Why do you ask?"

"I can tell you have an incredible body."

"You're making me blush."

"I doubt you're the blushing type," I said.

Slowly, we both stopped smiling. He took my hand and slipped it beneath the hem of his shirt, the movement slow and unhurried. Warm skin met my palm as I smoothed my hand over his solid flesh. His muscles tightened, reacting to my touch. I inhaled softly, my eyes locked on his as he watched me the entire time.

I eased my hand across the ridges of his abdomen and then

inched upward, the faint rasp of his chest hairs grazing my fingers.

"You're staring," I murmured.

"So are you."

My thumb traced the edge of his pec and encountered the steady thudding of his heart beneath bone and muscle. Much faster than before.

He stepped closer, erasing the small space between us. My hand remained under his shirt, trapped between us and pressed against his chest. Without breaking eye contact, he lifted the bottle of beer from my other hand and placed it on the counter.

"You were making a comment about my body."

"Was I?"

"Yeah. You said something about it being incredible?"

"Oh yeah," I breathed. My body throbbed with longing. I tilted my lips higher, desperate for him to kiss me.

His eyes became heavy-lidded as they dipped to my lips. "I can't concentrate when I'm so close to you."

"Then stop trying."

A smile ghosted his mouth, and his hand slid to the small of my back, urging me closer until the tips of my breasts pressed into his chest. The tension between us cracked and coiled tighter.

But just as he started lowering his head, a knock sounded at the door.

Marcus paused, his eyes locked on my parted lips, my entire body tight with anticipation.

He cursed softly and reluctantly pulled back. "I need to get that. It's probably our food."

Disappointed, I slipped my hand from under his shirt. He went to the door, and sure enough, a man stood outside with our pizza. I picked up my beer and moved to the table, and when Marcus brought over the pizza, we sat down to eat.

The hunger we had felt for each other transferred to the food. Marcus told me the restaurant was a spot a couple of miles away that he frequented because they had great prices and the food was delicious, and he wasn't kidding. Half pepperoni and half sausage, it was genuinely the best pizza I'd ever had.

We talked as we ate about all sorts of topics. This wasn't the fancy date I had envisioned when he first asked me out, but I believed it was just as good in a different way—comfortable and relaxing without the formality of a fine dining restaurant.

I learned a lot about him as we chatted. We both enjoyed the outdoors—hiking, fishing, camping—and I also learned that he skied, something I had never personally tried. He had attended Black Ski Weekend in Colorado for the past five years straight, though he admitted he wasn't only going for the skiing.

He was originally from Atlanta, where his parents and sisters currently lived with their families. I told him I was the youngest of four and that my parents had passed away a few years apart. My siblings all lived in other states, but we kept in touch through a family group chat.

After we finished eating, we moved to the living room, and Marcus turned on Netflix.

"What are you in the mood for? Action, drama..."

"Let's watch a romantic comedy."

"Whatever the lady wants."

After sliding through a few options, he selected a movie and clicked start.

"Oh, I almost forgot. I wanted to show you the ties Noah and I chose. I'll be right back." He left the room and returned with five ties.

"These are nice. I love this one," I said, holding up the tie with Batman and Robin on it.

"As soon as he saw that one, he practically screamed with joy. I had to buy it."

"And with these other two, you both match. How sweet."

"That's what he wanted. I figure in another couple of weeks we can buy more ties if he's interested."

"I'm sure he will be." I placed the ties on the table in front of us. "But, um, you're talking like someone who expects to have Noah here for the long term."

"Yeah." He rubbed his hands together. "I'm going to keep him."

My eyes widened. "When did you decide this?"

"The night he ran away. He trusts me, Julia, and I can't let him down."

"Is that the only reason?" I asked gently.

"Nah. He hasn't lived with me very long, but I can't imagine my life without him anymore. He's more than my little buddy. He's..." He searched for the right word.

"Your son?" I supplied.

"Yeah," he said, nodding slowly.

"You know what I think? Brandon and Stacey knew you better than you knew yourself. They knew you would take care of their son like he was your own, and that's why they chose you as his guardian—over anyone else in their family, including his Aunt Zenobia in Tennessee. No matter what shortcomings you thought you had, they saw right through you and knew you were the right person."

He stretched a hand across the back of the sofa and played with a strand of my hair. "There you go again, trying to make me blush."

I leaned in and kissed his bearded cheek, the hairs on his jaw gently scraping my lips. We snuggled together, me resting right under his arm. Then he kissed my temple, and I contentedly relaxed against him to watch the movie.

Chapter 15

Julia

"Wake up, sleepyhead."

I blinked as I woke up. What the heck?

I had dozed off. I remembered enjoying the movie, but I guess I had become so comfortable in Marcus's arms that I fell asleep.

Sitting up, I covered my mouth as I yawned. "What time is it?"

"Almost eleven."

"Late. Where's your bathroom? I need to splash some water on my face."

He directed me to the hall bathroom, and I closed the door quietly behind me. I briefly splashed water on my face to wake myself up. Then I exited to find Marcus sitting on the arm of the sofa.

"You awake now?" he asked with amusement.

"Yes. Did you watch the whole movie?" I asked, surprised.

"Honestly?"

"Yes, honestly."

"I fell asleep too."

"I knew it!"

I smacked his chest, and he caught my wrist, pulling me between his thighs. His other hand moved to the small of my back, and I leaned into the heat radiating from his body.

"I should go," I said quietly.

"Why?"

"It's late."

His thumb drew circles on the inside of my wrist. "I don't want you to go. Stay."

He looked at me as if I were a precious object. I couldn't remember the last time a man had looked at me in the same way. I knew what he was asking.

"What about Noah?" I asked, resting my hands on his shoulders.

"You're gonna have to be quiet so you don't wake him up."

I arched an eyebrow. "Me? Maybe you'll be the one hollering."

He chuckled.

"You think I'm being funny?"

"You're cute. I don't holler. I make women holler." He kissed my chin. "Will you stay?"

"Yes. I'll stay."

His lips found mine in a kiss filled with desire and promise, breaking away to stand and lead me down the hallway to his bedroom.

He closed the door quietly, and then his hands were on me again, sliding my shirt over my head. We quickly removed our clothes, tossing them haphazardly around the room. There was no awkward fumbling, just two people intent on finally exploring the chemistry between us.

When we were both naked, he backed me toward the bed, and my knees hit the mattress. I sat down and leaned back on my hands to look up at him.

His body was magnificent. Golden brown skin covered muscles in his thighs, torso, and arms.

"You're so damn beautiful," he whispered in a rough voice.

He joined me on the bed and pushed me back onto the pillows, his mouth finding mine again and kissing me with a deep, searching exploration. He caressed my breasts and traced the curves of my waist and hips. When I reached between us to stroke his length, he groaned against my lips.

Skin on skin, we explored each other. His warm, solid body moved on top of mine as his hands slid over the expanse of my stomach to the swell of my breasts. When his mouth closed over one nipple, I gasped, arching my back and grabbing onto the back of his head. He lavished it with attention, licking and sucking until I was writhing beneath him.

He rolled onto his back and pulled me on top of him. Straddling him, with my thighs bracketing his hips, the hard length of his erection pressed against my core. His large hands spanned my waist, and he looked up at me with something akin to reverence in his eyes.

"Look at you," he murmured, sliding his hands higher to cup my breasts. His thumbs brushed over the sensitive peaks, and I arched into his touch, my fingers curling into the soft cotton sheets. "You're perfect."

I leaned down to kiss him, my thick hair falling forward and creating a curtain around us. He made a masculine sound of approval deep in his throat, smoothing his hands over my hips, my back, and my thighs.

As the kiss deepened, I ground my pelvis against his, and we both moaned.

"Now. Please," I whispered.

He directed me to the nightstand with his eyes, and I reached over and removed a condom from the drawer. I put it on him, my fingers lingering on the task. I took pleasure in hearing him groan and watching as he bit into his bottom lip.

When he was finally covered, he placed his hands on my hips and guided me onto his length. I sank down onto him, and we both moaned. The stretch was exquisite, the fullness exactly what I needed.

I didn't move at first, simply allowing my body to adjust to his size.

"You good?" he asked in a strained voice.

"Yes," I breathed.

I began to move then, finding a rhythm that made us both lose our breath. His hands continued to roam over my body—up my sides, cupping my breasts and squeezing them, then going lower again to hold onto my hips and guide my movements.

Neither of us spoke. We didn't need to. We communicated with our bodies and the sound of our breathing. As the pressure built between us, I paid attention to his expressions as I rode him. I watched the way his jaw clenched and the way his eyes darkened with pleasure. He was beautifully unguarded as he shared his raw reactions.

"Julia, *goddamn.*" His hands tightened on my hips. "Baby, I need..."

I gyrated my hips as I bounced up and down on his hard dick.

He suddenly dropped an F-bomb and then flipped us over, never breaking our connection. One minute I was on top, the next I was on my back with him above me. He positioned my leg higher on his hip and switched the angle. I cried out and sank my nails into his biceps.

He lowered his head to my ear. "Shh," he said, reminding me that we weren't alone.

Each successive thrust was deliberately deep and slow, and

his mouth was everywhere—on my lips, on my neck, on my collarbone. His hands were too, continuing to torture me and moving all over my body.

Pressure coiled tighter inside me until I felt as if I were suffocating. I could barely think. All I could do was feel his hard body thrusting into mine. My fingers dug into the muscles of his back, and my legs wrapped around him, pulling him deeper as my hips bounced frantically faster.

"That's it, baby," he murmured in my ear. "Go on ahead and let go, Julia. I got you."

And so I did. The orgasm crashed over me, wave after wave hitting me and forcing my body to arch and tremble beneath him. Another loud cry burst from my lungs as my head tossed back. I couldn't help it. He felt *so damn* good.

Seconds later, his rhythm faltered and he buried his face in my neck, releasing my name as a rough whisper while his fingers sank into my hips and dragged me tighter against him.

He shattered against me, releasing a loud, breathless groan as he climaxed. Panting hard, he collapsed on top of me, spent from the power of his own orgasm.

We stayed in the same position for a while, our hearts pounding, both of us breathing hard. The sheets were twisted around my feet, and we were lying diagonally across the bed.

Finally, Marcus rolled off of me, and we both stared up at the ceiling.

"Wow," I whispered.

He laughed softly. "Yeah. Wow."

A few minutes later, after he had disposed of the condom in the adjoining bathroom, we pulled the covers over our naked bodies and snuggled together. I rested my head on his chest and listened to the steady beat of his heart.

Closing my eyes, I allowed myself to drift in the warmth of Marcus's arms—content and completely satisfied.

Chapter 16

Julia

I woke slowly, awareness creeping across my consciousness as I rolled onto my back on an impossibly comfortable mattress. Marcus's lingering scent remained in the air around me, and I smiled.

Marcus.

Memories of last night came rushing back. The way he kissed me. The firm pressure of his hands on my skin, and the way my body responded to his every touch. Moaning quietly, I turned onto my side, sensing I was alone in bed and wishing I wasn't.

Except I wasn't alone.

When I opened my eyes, Noah was standing beside the bed in his pajamas, staring at me with curious eyes.

"Ohmigod!" I yelped, clutching the sheet up to my neck.

How long had he been standing there?

"Good morning, Miss Julia," he said, completely unfazed in the way only a child could be.

"Hi. Good morning, Noah." My gaze flitted around the room, hoping Marcus would suddenly appear, but I didn't hear him in the adjoining bathroom. "Where is your Uncle Marcus?"

"He went to get breakfast. He told me to be quiet because you were still asleep."

Clearly, he forgot to tell Noah the most important part—do not come into this room. You have to be very specific when you give instructions to children.

"Well, you did a very good job because I had no idea you were standing beside the bed," I said.

"Did you and Uncle Marcus have a sleepover?" Noah asked, his head tilting to the side.

Sleepover. Cute.

"Um... yes, we did."

"Did you play the tickle game?"

"The what?"

"The tickle game. Sometimes Uncle Marcus plays it with me when he puts me to bed, and I can't stop screaming and laughing, and I mess up the sheets."

"Oh, um... yeah, we did play the tickle game. There was some screaming, and the sheets definitely got messed up."

"Uncle Marcus is really good at the tickle game," Noah said in a matter-of-fact voice.

"He sure is."

I heard the front door open and close, followed by footsteps in the hallway. Marcus eased open the door, perhaps thinking I was still asleep. He took in the scene with me clutching the sheet like a lifeline and Noah standing beside the bed.

His eyes widened. "Hey, buddy. Let's give Miss Julia some privacy."

"But we were talking about the tickle game."

Marcus frowned in confusion.

"I told him we played last night during our sleepover," I said.

"Oh. Right. Yeah, we played twice last night, didn't we?" His face shifted into amusement. "Okay, big man. Let's go into the kitchen and give Miss Julia some privacy."

He scooped up Noah and carried him out, closing the door behind them. I covered my face and laughed. Then I rolled out of bed and went into the bathroom. After washing my face and rinsing out my mouth, I finger-combed my hair into some semblance of order and then I started hunting for my clothes.

One by one, I found them strewn across the room and slipped them on. As I was closing the snap on my jeans, Marcus knocked and then came in, closing the door behind him. He leaned against it, an apologetic but amused expression on his face.

"I'm sorry. I ran next door to buy breakfast, and he was already awake when I was on my way out. He saw your purse in the living room and asked about you, so I explained you were here but sleeping—and *not* to bother you or make any noise. Clearly, he did the opposite."

"It's fine."

A lazy smile appeared on his lips. "Good morning."

I sauntered over to where he stood and allowed him to fold me into his arms. "Good morning."

He kissed the tip of my nose and then my lips. "I bought sausage, egg, and cheese sandwiches on bagels. They're my favorite. Coffee too, if you're interested."

"Sounds divine."

He kissed me again and slapped my bottom. "I like these jeans," he murmured.

I whimpered and pressed my face into his neck, taking a deep inhale to drag the intoxicating scent of him into my lungs. "Okay, enough. I need food," I said.

He chuckled. "Right this way."

Noah was already at the table, his legs swinging as he ate a hash brown. "Miss Julia, Uncle Marcus got a lot of food so you can eat too."

"That was so nice of him." I took the chair across from him, and Marcus handed me a sandwich and a large coffee. He grabbed sugar from the cabinet and cream from the fridge and then sat down at the table with us.

We ate breakfast together, like a domestic unit, and the moment stirred emotion inside me. I used to believe I never wanted this life, but sitting and talking with Marcus and Noah as we ate breakfast changed my perspective. I wouldn't mind doing this every Sunday morning.

The funniest part was, Marcus and I didn't have to say much. Noah dominated the conversation with factoids and lots of questions. Watching them together was also very sweet. They had an easy affection between them, and Marcus was patient and loving with Noah, alternating between answering his questions and asking questions of his own. He wiped crumbs from the boy's mouth and showed such gentleness that a dangerous yearning tightened my chest.

Maybe I wanted this life after all. Or maybe it wasn't that I necessarily wanted a family as much as I wanted *this* family. I had fallen for both Marcus and Noah and wanted to be a part of their lives in a substantial way.

I finished my food and helped Marcus clear the table. I was reluctant to leave, but I needed to take a shower and had to go home at some point.

Noah plopped down on the sofa to watch cartoons, and Marcus walked me to the door.

"Last night was amazing," he said in a low voice, cupping my jaw and looking deeply into my eyes. "I want to see you again. I want to keep seeing you."

"You're really different, you know that?"

"How?"

"You wouldn't believe how much men play games and don't say exactly what they want. But you're direct, and I appreciate it."

"I don't want there to be any confusion about what I'm looking for. So what do you think? You and me...?"

"You've been direct with me, so I'll be direct with you. Yes, I'm definitely interested, and I want to see where this can go." I placed a hand on his chest. "You're nothing like I thought, Marcus. When I first met you, I assumed you were a player. The Romeo license plate tipped me off. But now that I've gotten to know you better, there's a little bit of Romeo—yes—but there's quite a bit of Batman and Marcus too. A nice blend of all three."

"Human beings are complex."

"Yes, we are," I agreed.

His thumb stroked my cheek. "You're okay with group dates for a while?"

"I am. Just call me."

I lifted onto my toes and kissed him briefly. Then I peered around him to catch sight of Noah. "Bye-bye, Noah."

He jumped off the sofa and ran over, his bare feet slapping on the hardwood floor. I bent down and gave him a hug and kissed the top of his head.

"Bye," he said, gazing up at me and waving.

I left the two of them in the doorway. The elevator ride down felt endless, and my insides felt as if they were being torn apart. I used to say I didn't want to be a mother, but now I could see myself being a surrogate mother, at least. Little Noah had stolen my heart, the same way his godfather did.

I drove home with the radio on, singing at the top of my lungs so I wouldn't be consumed by my thoughts. When I entered my apartment, the silence hit me. Leanne and the girls had already left. There were no toys scattered on the floor, and I couldn't hear the distant sound of children's laughter.

The silence had never been this loud.

I found a note from her on the table behind the sofa.

Thanks for everything. I guess the date went well? Call me. I want all the details!

I replaced the piece of paper on the table and stood in my pristine living room with everything in its place. I was completely alone. I almost turned around and ran back to Noah and Marcus, where they were both probably sitting on the sofa watching cartoons.

The two of them had changed my outlook on life and reshaped my expectations for the future. I no longer pictured myself as a woman alone in her apartment. I wanted the chaos of family—the noise, the mess, and the kind of love that ran deeply.

I hadn't gone searching for it, and now that I'd acknowledged my new vision for the future, I hoped Marcus didn't disappoint me.

Because in my thirty-three years of life, he was the only man who had ever made me want that life. He would either become the best decision I ever made or the worst.

Only time would tell which.

Chapter 17

Marcus

Levy Park was packed with families on Saturday afternoon, but the members of the Single Dad Society were easy to find. The dads, a mix of different races—but mostly Black—crowded into one area.

Some sat together at the picnic tables while others kept an eye on the kids playing frisbee and kickball. Other kids ran around the playground, playing on the swings and careening down the slide—their screams of joy filling the morning air.

The society had rented the pavilion, so as Noah and I approached, a couple of the fathers were busy working the grill, cooking hot dogs and hamburgers.

"Uncle Marcus, look!" Noah pointed excitedly at the splash fountain where children were running through the water.

"I guess you want to do that, huh?"

"Can I?"

We were here so I could meet other men in my situation, and he could make new friends. "Yeah, go on."

He raced away without looking back.

I spotted my frat brothers Elijah and Jashaun sitting at a table. They saw me at the same time, and Elijah waved me over.

"About time you showed up, man," he said.

Elijah, whose line name was Enforcer because of his strict adherence to following the rules, was solidly built with honey-colored eyes and golden brown skin. Jashaun, whose line name was Ocean because of his ability to go with the flow or make it rough for anyone who pushed him too hard, was of average build.

I gave them both some dap before dropping onto the bench beside Jashaun. "I had to stop at the real estate office before I came."

"I guess that was Noah?" Elijah asked, nodding his head toward the splash fountain.

"One and the same. I would've introduced you guys, but he was eager to get over there and get wet."

"I hope you came prepared to have your seats soaked," Jashaun said.

I tapped my temple. "I was thinking ahead. Inside this backpack is an extra change of clothes." I tapped the bag and then placed it on the grass beside me.

"Look at you, thinking like a parent," Elijah said.

"Got to. I've had a crash course the past couple of months. Where are your kids?"

"Sabrina's over there doing cartwheels," Elijah replied, pointing.

I saw a pretty little girl with braids performing impressive moves. She was bigger than the last time I saw her. Kids grew so fast. "You have a gymnast on your hands," I remarked.

"Yeah. She hasn't stopped doing cartwheels since she learned how." Elijah shook his head as we laughed.

"My daughter, Jussica, is over there playing kickball, in the blue shorts and striped shirt," Jashaun said. He elbowed me. "The bruhs asked about you at The Flight Club. I told them you were busy and would be back once your life calms down."

The Flight Club was the spot for our monthly graduate chapter networking meetups.

"Thanks, man. I think it'll be at least another month before I feel comfortable enough leaving Noah with anyone at night. The only person I think could even pull it off is his child advocate, Julia."

"The one you've been sleeping with?" Jashaun asked.

"You don't have to be so blunt."

"Am I wrong?"

"No, you're not," I reluctantly grumbled.

"A'ight then."

He and Elijah had a good laugh at my expense.

For the past couple of weeks, Julia and I had been spending a lot of time together, so I gave her a drawer in my dresser and space in my closet. It made sense since she was always at the condo. A couple of nights a week, she came over after work and had dinner with me and Noah, usually something I picked up on the way home. She spent the weekends with us too, and each Sunday cooked us a delicious home-cooked meal.

My own cooking skills were slowly improving. Pop-Tarts were no longer on the breakfast menu since fixing a meal was a lot easier than I initially thought. If you could read a recipe, you could probably cook. My spaghetti and meatballs were a hit with Noah, but I was concentrating on breakfast meals. I created my own version of the sausage, egg, and cheese sandwiches I liked to buy on the weekends and had mastered making breakfast burritos, which Noah especially loved. Yesterday, I made a frittata for the first time—another win. Noah and I ate the rest of it for breakfast this morning with fruit on the side.

"So Noah's therapy is going well?" Elijah peered around Jashaun to ask the question.

"Yeah, which is why I think leaving him might be easier in another month or so. Maybe less. That's the feedback the therapist is giving me concerning his abandonment issues. They've spent a lot of time discussing his fears in therapy."

"What are you going to do about his aunt?" Elijah asked.

I inwardly groaned. With Julia's help, I had filled out the guardianship paperwork, and she had closed the case on Noah, but the attorney received notice that Zenobia was contesting the legality of my guardianship over Noah.

"She's become a pain," I said, rubbing my hand over my face, exhaustion settling in when I thought about what she had done. "She filed a petition to challenge my guardianship, claiming that as his biological aunt, she has more right to him than I do. Noah should be with 'blood family.' Real family."

"Brandon and Stacey named you as his guardian. That has to mean something," Jashaun said, sounding appalled.

"I know, and their wishes are documented in the guardianship papers and their will, all filed years ago." My gaze settled on Noah splashing through the fountain with the other kids, their laughter traveling across the park. "The attorney says I have a strong case, but her attorney is arguing that blood relation should take precedence, and Zenobia and her husband can provide a 'traditional family environment.'"

"Bullshit," Elijah said forcefully. "What the hell does a traditional family environment have to do with anything if the kid is happy and healthy with you?"

I sighed. "Not a damn thing, but I know why she's really fighting for custody."

"The money," Elijah said.

"What money?" Jashaun asked.

I had mentioned the insurance money to Elijah but hadn't

yet told Jashaun. I proceeded to explain about the million-dollar policy payout. "Zenobia even mentioned that I'm not capable of properly managing his inheritance."

"But she is?"

"Yeah." My shoulders slumped.

"How confident are you in your attorney's ability to help you keep Noah?" Jashaun asked.

I shrugged. "He's an estate attorney, so handling the paperwork was easy. Now that the guardianship is being contested, I'm cautiously hopeful but... worried."

I couldn't lose Noah. He was an integral part of my life. He was *my* kid—legally and in my heart.

"When is your court date?" Jashaun asked.

"In three weeks."

"Hang on a sec." He stood and turned to the men at the grill. "Hey, Eric! Come here for a minute." He returned his attention to me. "Eric is one of the state's top litigators and specializes in contested custody and guardianship cases. When this goes to trial, you need someone like him who lives in family court."

A tall brother in his early forties walked over wearing an apron. His close-cropped hair was graying at the temples, giving him the confident bearing of someone who spent a lot of time in courtrooms.

Jashaun introduced us, and I stood to shake his hand. Then I gave him the condensed version of my problems with Zenobia and my desire to keep Noah. "As far as the life insurance payout is concerned," I said, finishing up, "I've already started the paperwork to set up a trust for Noah's future. I have a successful career and my own money. I don't need it."

Eric had been listening intently, and when I finished, he said, "Sounds like a pretty solid case to me. The biological relationship does give the aunt standing to petition, but it doesn't automatically override *your* rights. The court will look at a number of points: The parents' clearly expressed wishes to have you as the child's guardian, Noah's current well-being and stability in your care, whether moving him to Tennessee is too disruptive, the aunt's motivation and historical relationship with the child, and your plans for the insurance money. The fact that you've started setting up a trust shows you're thinking about Noah's long-term interests."

"So you think I can beat her?" I asked.

"You should, but family court is unpredictable. There are no guarantees. You need good representation."

"That's why I called you over here. I know you're the best and can help my man out," Jashaun said.

"But you already have an attorney," Eric said.

"I do, but—"

"That don't mean nothing," Elijah said from his position on the bench. "You said yourself he needs good representation, and no one's better than you."

Eric chuckled. "I'm good, but no one is invincible. I'm ninety-nine percent sure you'll be able to keep your boy. Which one is he?"

I pointed. Noah had left the fountain area and was playing tag with some of the other kids. "Yellow shirt."

"He looks happy," Eric remarked. "Tell you what, take my number and call on Monday to set up a consultation. Tell the receptionist who answers that you're with the Single Dad Society. She knows to put those calls through directly to me. I'll review your case, no charge for an initial review. If you decide to work with me, you'll receive the single dad discount."

He rattled off the number, and I plugged the digits into my phone. "Thanks, man." I shook his hand again.

"No problem. You're one of us now. We have to look out for each other." He clapped me on the shoulder and walked away.

Relief washing over me, I sat down.

"He's being modest," Jashaun said, reclaiming his seat as well. "I heard he's never lost a case he took on for any of the single fathers in the organization."

"I heard the same thing," Elijah said. "One of the dads in the Austin chapter hired him during a custody battle. Think his name was John. Anyway, John was a dick and cheated on his wife, so she was getting back at him by keeping the kids away and fighting for sole custody. When Eric got finished, John had primary physical custody, and she ended up having to pay him child support."

"No way," I said.

"I'm not kidding. The man just wanted time with his kids, but turns out she worked a lot, including travel, and made way more money than John. Eric argued for stability for the kids and said it was better for John to have primary custody."

"Damn. He's good," I murmured.

I didn't expect Zenobia to back down easily with a million dollars at stake, but as I sat on the bench watching Noah play like the fun-loving seven-year-old he was meant to be, I was hopeful. More than hopeful. I was extremely optimistic.

Brandon had entrusted me with his son if the worst ever happened, and unfortunately, the worst did. Since then, I had truly become Noah's parent and was no longer stumbling through my new role. I had embraced it and savored it.

Noah was all I had left of my best friend, my brother. I loved him as if he was my own. And I was going to fight like hell to hold onto him.

Chapter 18

Marcus

"After careful consideration of the evidence presented, including the testimony of the minor child, the court finds that it is in Noah Mitchell's best interest to remain in the care of Marcus Hayes, his legally designated guardian."

The judge's voice boomed in the courtroom, each word landing with the weight of finality. Then he continued, "The petitioner has failed to demonstrate that removing the child from his current placement would serve his welfare. Mr. Hayes has provided stable, loving care, and Noah has formed a significant bond with him. The original guardianship designation made by the deceased parents will stand. This court's ruling is final."

The gavel came down with a sharp crack, and air rushed from my lungs, relief hitting me so hard my body sagged forward, and my head dropped into my hands.

Noah was staying with me. He was mine.

Eric clapped a hand on my shoulder and squeezed. "Congratulations, Marcus. You did it."

I lifted my head as a small, softer hand squeezed my other shoulder from behind.

Julia.

Across the aisle, Zenobia shot me a look of pure venom before muttering something to her attorney. She gathered her belongings with sharp, angry movements and stormed out of the courtroom.

I didn't care how angry she was. Noah was staying with me. That was all that mattered.

I gripped Eric's hand. "Thank you," I said, which seemed insufficient after what he had accomplished.

"You don't have to thank me. You had a strong case, and you're a good father." He began to pack up his briefcase. "My office will file the final paperwork next week, and I'll have a courier send over a copy for your records."

After he left, I stood and faced Julia. She reached for me, and I pulled her into my arms in the middle of the aisle, crushing her to me. I was probably holding on too tight, but having her soft body pressed against me grounded me after the stress of the trial. Fear and exhaustion were emotions of the past. Only overwhelming relief remained.

We held each other for a little longer as the courtroom emptied, and then I finally pulled back. "We should go get him. He's been waiting out there long enough."

Hand in hand, we exited the courtroom and found Noah in the hall sitting next to Mrs. Patterson, an older woman wearing a hat and glasses. He wore a suit, and his tie—royal blue and gold—matched the one I wore under my jacket.

As soon as we appeared, his anxious eyes searched our faces for answers. He had testified, sitting in the chair at the front of the courtroom and answering questions. The judge had been kind, but I knew the entire experience had scared Noah. I had to sit quietly in my chair, unable to protect him, with a neutral expression on my face while my insides twisted into knots. After his testimony, they removed him from the courtroom, and he had been waiting out here ever since with the babysitter, neither of them knowing what the outcome would be.

"Ready to go home?" I asked.

For half a beat, he seemed dazed. Then his face crumpled, and he launched himself off the bench and into my arms. I lifted him from the floor, and he wrapped his arms around me. Then he started crying, releasing all the pent-up emotion he had been holding inside.

He might not have understood everything that was taking place, but he understood enough to be afraid and know he might lose what was familiar to him—again.

"It's okay," I whispered, cradling the back of his head. "We're going home, buddy. Together."

Noah sniffed. "I thought..." His voice broke. "I thought she was gonna take me to Tennessee."

"She can't. You're staying with me forever." I kissed his temple. "I promise. That's not changing. Okay?"

He nodded and wiped the tears from his cheeks.

Mrs. Patterson dabbed at her eyes with a tissue. "Congratulations, Marcus. This is what Brandon and Stacey wanted."

"I appreciate you being here," I said sincerely.

"Of course. Any time you need me." She smiled and said goodbye to all of us.

Noah had stopped crying, but he still clung to me, so I didn't put him down. Real talk, I didn't want to. We headed toward the exit—me, Noah, and Julia.

Walking together into our future.

Noah screamed, laughing, twisting, and turning on the bed as I attacked his ribs. His laughter bounced off the walls—one of my favorite sounds in the world.

"Uncle Marcus, stop!" he choked out.

I finally quit, and he settled down.

"You're gonna be good now?" I asked.

"Yes, I promise," he said, still giggling.

When I had told him it was time for bed, he had sassed me back and said he was going to bed when he wanted to. I chased him around the condo and into his bedroom, where he slipped under the covers, prompting one of our tickle fights. It wasn't much of a fight since I always won.

I straightened the sheets around him.

"Are we going shopping for camping stuff tomorrow?" he asked.

"Yes. I have to work first, though, so you'll spend the day with Miss Julia. She's going to the supermarket to pick up a few items for dinner. When I get back, we'll buy your camping gear, okay?"

"I want a Robin sleeping bag," he said.

"We'll see if we can find one," I said. If they didn't have one at the store, I could probably find one online.

He grinned at me. "Can I have my own water thing? What's it called?"

I knew exactly what he was doing by asking questions, purposely trying to stay up later. "A canteen. But you know what? If you keep asking questions, we won't go shopping for any camping gear, and Miss Julia and I will go camping without you. Then we'll leave you here in the condo all by yourself."

"No!" he shrieked, laughing.

"Yes. Now go to sleep."

He squeezed his eyes shut.

"Perfect. Good night. Love you." I kissed his forehead and stood.

As I reached for the light, I heard him say, "Uncle Marcus?"

"Yeah, buddy?"

"I love you too."

I smiled. "See you in the morning." I turned out the light and eased the door shut.

Julia was in the kitchen putting away the leftovers from dinner. I walked up behind her as she was snapping the lid on one of the containers. Slipping my arms around her waist, I kissed the curve of her neck.

"Is he asleep?" she asked.

"He will be in a few minutes."

She turned and looped her arms around my neck. "What time will you be finished with work tomorrow?"

"Let's see... I have two listing appointments in the morning. Then I need to check on a couple of empty properties. My buyer's assistants are handling the showings, so I should be free by mid-afternoon."

"Then we can go look for camping gear. Ever since you told Noah we're going camping, he hasn't stopped talking about it."

I let out a quiet laugh. "He just asked me about going to buy the gear while I was tucking him in. I'm still learning that I need to be careful what I mention to him because he never forgets."

"No, he doesn't."

Silence settled between us as I looked down into her dark eyes. "I couldn't have done this without you."

"Yes, you could have, but it might have been a lot less enjoyable."

"No doubt." I kissed her, tasting the softness of her lips. I ran my hands over the curve of her spine. "Ready for bed?"

"Mhmm. Let me put this last dish away."

I watched as she placed the last container in the refrigerator. She had been my calm in the middle of a storm. Steady. My rock. Her presence truly made everything better. That's why, now that the custody ordeal was behind me, I was going ring shopping next week. I wanted to marry her. I had already told Jashaun and Elijah my intentions, and they were happy for me.

I wanted Julia permanently in my life and Noah's. Despite what she'd said about not wanting to be a mother, recent conversations confirmed she had changed her mind. She loved Noah, too, and she loved me. I wanted us to be a family.

"Have I told you lately that I love you?" I asked.

"No," she said softly.

"I do. I love you so damn much."

Her hand caressed my jaw. "I love you too."

How did I get so lucky?

I kissed her again, but deeper this time, lifting her off her feet. She wrapped her legs around my waist and gently stroked the nape of my neck. Her touch was both an aphrodisiac and soothing.

As I walked with her in my arms toward the bedroom, I marveled at how much my life had changed in the past few months. I had been living in a vacuum, hopping from bed to bed, not realizing how empty my existence was and what I had been missing.

By terrible chance, my world changed when Noah became my responsibility. Then I met this woman in my arms, who made a tough, winding road easier to navigate.

I had outgrown my old life and become the man I was today. I still had a lot to learn, but I was confident that with her by my side, anything was possible.

Single Dad Society series

Meet the other single dads finding love in the Single Dad Society series.

OCEAN by Tiye

Known for making waves since his college days, Jashaun "Ocean" Howard, relishes being single and has no interest in sharing his world with anyone. Until he runs into an old fling and notices her daughter with a birthmark like his.

And his whole controlled life turns upside down when Ocean is unexpectedly thrust into fatherhood.

As Ocean navigates raising a headstrong child who immediately captures his heart, he is inexplicably drawn to his hot neighbor who seems frustratingly immune to his charms. Until she isn't.

For a man who wouldn't trade his freedom for anything, he never expected love to be his everything.

ENFORCER by Synithia Williams

After Elijah "Enforcer" Holmes is blindsided by his wife's request for a divorce he's left with sole custody of their young daughter. He's always lived by the rules and values instilled in him by his traditional parents. Rules he follows even harder now to give his daughter the stability she needs. But living by the rules has left him little time to find joy. Except when it comes to Layla Townsend, the mother of his daughter's best friend. He doesn't want to ruin their friendship, but there's something about her smile that makes him yearn for more.

Layla divorced her ex-husband because he treated her more like a personal assistant than a partner. Now a single mother, she's not willing to sacrifice her peace for anyone. Even a man as enticing as Elijah. She's ignored the attraction simmering between them, but when Elijah decides to bend the rules and prove to her they'd be the perfect pair, she's ready to discover if breaking his rules is worth the risk.

* * *

Free short stories and the full catalogue of Delaney Diamond's books are available at delaneydiamond.com.

About the Author

Delaney Diamond is the USA Today Bestselling Author of sensual, passionate romance novels. Originally from the U.S. Virgin Islands, she now lives in Atlanta, Georgia. She reads romance novels, mysteries, thrillers, and a fair amount of nonfiction. When she's not busy reading or writing, she's in the kitchen trying out new recipes, dining at one of her favorite restaurants, or traveling to an interesting locale.

Enjoy free reads on her website. Join her mailing list to get sneak peeks, notices of sale prices, and find out about new releases.

Join her mailing list
www.delaneydiamond.com

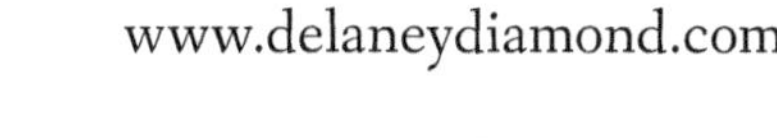
instagram.com/delaneydiamondbooks

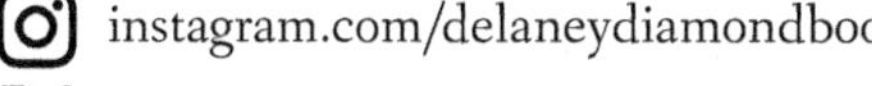
x.com/DelaneyDiamond

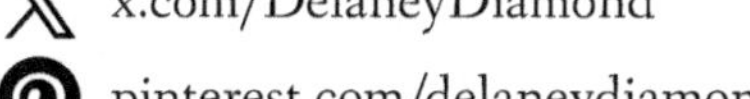
pinterest.com/delaneydiamond

www.ingramcontent.com/pod-product-compliance
Lightning Source LLC
LaVergne TN
LVHW010104110826
845155LV00028B/471

* 9 7 8 1 9 4 6 3 0 2 3 5 9 *